CANTERBURY MURDERS

G.C. FISHER

CONTENTS

Canterbury Murders.

By G.C. Fisher.

❀ Created with Vellum

FOREWORD

Sometimes when your world falls apart you are forced into that re-think you have been putting off for years. The pandemic did that for me, and this book is the result. It didn't start off as a book, that was too much of a challenge. It started off as a short story which I put on FaceBook. Thanks to the friends and family who bothered to read it and asked for more it grew. Without that it would have ended there. The story evolved with almost daily episodes egged on by an amazing group of people who engaged with the characters and drove me on. A debate over whether to read the daily chapter over a glass of wine in the evening or morning coffee gave me confidence that the readers were having a good time. Now it's done, the feedback has been included, and personal stories added. I hope you enjoy it too.

~

Sign up!

If you would like to hear more about Maeve and
..what's coming soon...
please sign up to the mailing list on
www.GCFisherAuthor.com

ACKNOWLEDGMENTS

This book would definitely not have happened without the following people. I am incredibly grateful to those who got involved on FaceBook, and those who shared their strange experiences, and particularly to the special advisors, readers and editors who picked up many errors. Story advisor and all round positive support Raoul Morris, advisor on all matters to do with the police and setting the world to rights Steve Swain and wonderfully picky editor Rachael Morris. Story readers, contributors, and 'egg-ers on', Alexandra Peers, Anne Gately, Anne Westcott, Avril Roundtree, Carla Morris, Carmilla Cardina, Caroline Morris, Catherine Droubaix, Christina Coleman, Corrie Jeffreys, Damian Morris, Emma Bewick, Gill Wilson, Jenny Hudson, Jane Kagon, Jean Stanton, Jenny Kos, Jenny Richardson, Kim Horsford, Maria Sheehy, Matthew Scott, Melise Nevin, Nathalie Milliken, Prof G.D. Jayalakshmi, Ruth Kelly, Sally Fegan-Wyles, Sandra Gray, Susan Mulhall, Victoria Bajic, Victoria Hamilton, Wendy Taylor, William Fegan.

CHAPTER 1

THE BEGINNING

Looking back, Maeve was never really sure if it was the fact of turning forty, or her bucket list of life altering decisions, that caused it. The one thing she was sure of, was the day on which it all started.

Maeve McPhillips was an ordinary person. And it all began on an ordinary day. A nice sunny late spring day. Maeve had agreed to take her mother, Ada, over to an event in Margate. So far so good. However, the event was a gathering of spiritual mediums. Ada was a medium, and this was one of the issues between them, Maeve thought it was simply a load of hokum, and she didn't approve of peddling hope to the desperate. Ada revelled in the drama of it, the more incense, candles, kohl-dark eyes and gold earrings the better. Ada did ouija boards and seances too.

In her state of sorting out her life, 'rephrasing' her relationship with Ada was one of the areas that Maeve wanted to work on. They had always had issues. Maeve blamed Ada's spiritual activities for her frequently being 'away with the fairies' and having missed out on a substantial amount of Maeve's childhood. She simply wasn't there for me, was Maeve's view when she was in a good mood. She didn't really love me, was her view when she was feeling sorry for herself.

So today was an attempt at a new beginning. Maeve had

just finished working on an event, a festival, and had some time. She had cleaned out the posters and accumulated rubbish from the car before picking Ada up. She managed the practicalities smoothly, they got there, and parked the car. They had enough time to debate between the 'Greedy Cow' or 'Curious Cupcake' cafes for their flat white in the centre of the old town. They headed back to the hall still in good time. Ada split off to collect her paraphernalia and Maeve went to take a seat at the back. The dry musty smell and the beeswax polish on the wooden seating, brought back many painful sessions of childhood misery to Maeve. She could hear the other attendees as they gathered. The tension of their desperation to communicate with someone who had passed over was palpable, they wanted a last message, or just the closure of a 'good-bye' that was never said. She lasted twenty minutes, but ultimately, Maeve couldn't take it.

She slipped out the door before the session got fully underway hoping that Ada wouldn't notice her missing. As she hit the sunlight she took a deep breath and felt free. Like one of those special days off school. Here she was in Margate, and now, for the next few hours her time was her own. With a quick march back through the Old Town Square, onto the Parade, she turned right towards the Turner Contemporary, and considered another coffee, or, a walk along the harbour arm and back with an ice cream as a reward? The air was fresh with that sea smell, and childhood memories of a creamy '99' won out.

Still working on her 'how to fix my life' list Maeve was preoccupied. The walk was doing her good and helping her focus. Under consideration were her two daughters.

At almost 18, Marianne, seemed to have passed through adolescence minus most of the predicted 'out-bursts', screaming matches, or tantrums, if pushed, she could occasionally do something flaky, but so far that was it. Maybe they were yet to come, or maybe Maeve hadn't given her the space she needed to really express herself. Had she made Marianne grow up too quickly? Since the divorce, Maeve often talked through whatever was on her mind with Marianne. Marianne probably needed a break, and Maeve would suggest that, ideally before it got too close to the exams.

Orla, whose 16th birthday was next month, was showing any number of teenage symptoms, she seemed to fling her things around her room but then tidy them up, so not too bad on the cleanliness front. Sometimes, she could have an irrational cadenza, however, they were short lived, and usually once the emotional bubble burst, and the issue was in the open, that was that, over. The primary irritant at the moment was Orla's incessant use of the 'why' question, almost as a battering ram. Maeve was pondering 'Does everything really have to have an explanation?' when she was interrupted by "Excuse me", then louder, "Excuse me".

It took Maeve a moment to realise that a woman on the pier was talking directly to her. Dressed up for a special 'day out' in a soft pink and grey dress, which was moving gently in the breeze, she had a matching pink hat clutched to her head, though the wind didn't seem strong enough to blow anything away.

"Would you mind?" She went on, "See that woman over there, the one with the two children and her husband?" Maeve did, and nodded.

"Would you mind telling her that I'm okay, I'm fine, not to worry, I'm happy over here." She waved her arms encompassing the pier and sea wall, and finished with "I'm her mother."

The little family group were sitting on the edge of the pier, feet dangling over the edge but not touching the water, they looked happy and were laughing. In fact they were sitting right in the middle of her way to the ice-cream van.

"No problem, I'm going that way." Maeve nodded and smiled wondering why the woman wouldn't do it herself; she probably wanted longer on her own. Right now, Maeve absolutely understood that.

Back to her musings on her daughters and how to talk to Orla. Her thoughts then flipped between Orla and Marianne, and drifted to herself. As part of her reassessment of life priorities, Maeve had already started doing Yoga and mindfulness sessions, so she wandered back purposefully not rushing, taking it all in, smelling, feeling, and trying *not* to think, it was doing her a lot of good. Time to just 'be'.

As Maeve reached the family she called out to them, and much like it had with her, it took a few 'excuse-me's' to get their attention. She spoke directly to the woman.

"Your mother asked me to tell you that she's fine and happy over there." And Maeve pointed to where she had seen her. As Maeve turned back, she noticed the colour had drained from the woman's face.

"Is this a joke? It's cruel. You shouldn't do this to people!!" Her eyes had filled with tears and the others were completely silent.

"I'm sorry, I don't understand." At a loss Maeve didn't know what to say, so just went on talking "she said, that's my daughter over there pointing to you, tell her I'm fine, not to worry, I'm happy over here. That's all".

"What did she look like?"

Maeve described the pink hat, the dress, the soft grey curls, a little bit of make-up, blue eye-shadow.... Shrieks, cries and

"Oh my God! You did see her! My mother died a year ago. You have no idea how much this means to me!"

The family merged into one large hug. After a lot more cries, tears, hugs and kisses, the mother turned to Maeve.

"I have been so sad, worried about her, thinking of her being all alone, I haven't been dealing with it at all well. I miss her. Most of all I get upset because I thought she was sad. Now I'm sure that she is happy, it's okay, she knew that I needed to hear that to be able to start healing. And today of all days, you know that they say 'there are no coincidences'? Well, we were due to go to see some special Medium today. I don't believe in them, my husband thought we should try it anyway, but I just couldn't face it. The day out, the sea air, and the kids were all doing a great job of distracting me. Then you came to us anyway. She must have known."

Her face had returned to its normal colour, the streaks in the mascara looked happy, honest, real.

Maeve was stunned,

"It's fine... Actually, I am having difficulty in believing that she wasn't really there. She still feels very close by and I am sensing that she is happy to see you happy."

Maeve had been looking around, half expecting to see the woman in the distance behind her, and now needed some space to process all of this. So she discreetly withdrew leaving the family happily engrossed in each other.

Making it back to the car, Maeve waited for Ada, watching the door as people filed out of the seminar lingering in small groups to finish conversations. She saw Ada leaving, touching people to give comfort, saying her good-byes. Then Ada looked around trying to find Maeve, who waved through the windscreen and began to get out of the car, but Ada looked straight passed her, stopped still and smiled. 'Still away with the fairies', Maeve thought as she turned, to follow her gaze. She could now see the lady in the pink, nodding, smiling, and pointing to Maeve. Ada turned towards her, their eyes connected. Ada smiled.

CHAPTER 2

THE WAY HOME

Looking from the outside there was nothing to tell you what had just happened. Maeve and her mother were just two ordinary women out for the day getting into the car to go home.

Ada got into the car and nodded as if they had just had a conversation.

"Shall we go? I'm exhausted! Looking forward to getting into the house and kicking off the shoes, pouring that well deserved glass of wine hopefully in time to watch the sun go down. We want to get going before we are caught in the traffic".

She was right, it gets sticky around rush hour even at the weekend.

Maeve was still in shock and didn't know what to say, so she just started the car, pulled out of the parking space, and moved into the one-way system. It was still hot enough to have the windows down and hear the sounds of early summer, seagulls and amusement arcade electronic jingles. Maeve waited till they were on the main road to Folkestone, where it was much quieter, the sea air had changed to green countryside with the smells of cow parsley and fresh cut grass. She had taken the coast road via Sandwich, because she knew it like the back of her hand, and they would be able to talk without fear of taking the wrong turning.

"What just happened?" Maeve was trying to keep the tone normal.

"What do you mean, love?"

This was just typical of Ada, she was completely avoiding the issue. Maeve had seen and spoken to a ghost! Was Ada trying to be evasive? It irritated Maeve.

"I mean, that woman was dead! She spoke to me and then she seemed to talk to you! In my very normal, very ordinary, everyday world, this doesn't happen, it just doesn't, so tell me what happened."

"Well dear, you have had a moment of realisation, that's all. Something has happened to you. Sometimes there is a day that has special meaning, or it can just be the right time, you know like an age thing. I don't think that today is a particular day? Or is it?"

Ada was veering from being patronising to obtuse. Or maybe Maeve was allowing her emotions to get in the way, and was not asking the right questions. The history of their relationship was likely to lead to misinterpretation, or at a minimum, over sensitivities on both sides.

One thing for sure, Maeve did not want to be patronised.

"I need more than that." She said, still trying to control her voice.

"Ah, I see. Yes, whatever the reason, you have changed, and now you need answers. Well, you have always been able to see and communicate with those who have passed over, and today you understood that." Ada's tone was normal, conversational.

"I haven't, it's never happened before, I don't have the gift!" Louder than intended, Maeve's upset and frustration was now clear.

"See, now you are getting angry again. That's what happened before when you were a child, so rather than cause an upset, I let you think that the spirits were real people. You didn't want to think that they were 'ghosts'. The other kids told you that ghosts were bad, evil or frightening. You wanted to be normal, just like your school friends, so I went along. Do you remember your little friend Katie? She used to come around after school when there was no one else around?"

"Yes, what about her." The answer was sharp.

"She was a spirit, poor little thing, just wanted a friend to play with. Like you, she was lonely. You suited each other. She wasn't looking for anything, and you didn't want to ask questions. Like any other kids of that age you both wanted to get on with having fun, sharing adventures, and having a laugh."

This was a shock.

"But she was real! She was my friend." Maeve was having difficulty processing this latest revelation.

"She was your friend. She was a sad soul who died on her own, I think it was carbon monoxide poisoning myself, because she always wanted the windows open. Katie was looking for a playmate, and you made her happy. She just needed to laugh, to feel that someone cared, and that she wasn't alone, then she could be at peace. And so she was."

Not knowing what to say Maeve focused on her need for some practical explanations.

"Okay, it's a lot for me to take in. I know that I have grown up with your world in the background, and you have gone on about it for as long as I can remember, but in the past I wasn't really listening. Now I need to know things. First, do the spirits find us or do we find them?"

"You were listening," Ada replied, "but you didn't want to believe, so you shut your ears and decided that I was a little touched."

Ada's answer was sharp and revealed how hurt she had been.

"Now, your question. There are ways to call those on the other side, you know this, because you know about seances and many other ways that people in this world try to call their loved ones. You attended lots of special sessions, you played at the back, or under the table, and didn't look because you didn't want to see!"

Her voice had the clear traces of the disappointment this had caused. Sighing, she went on,

"They also find you. Those who have a need will seek a 'friend' on this side, to help them solve whatever their problem is. You seem to be sensitive to unhappiness. The lady you met knew that you would make the effort to talk to her daughter, she was most grateful and wanted to say thank you but you didn't see her until you felt her unhappiness again. There may be other things that trigger it for you, and the more you do, the more things will trigger spirits. Word seems to spread in the spirit world, so don't be surprised if someone contacts you pretty soon."

They had left the side roads and joined the M20, Maeve always loved that stretch of the M20 at the tunnel bypassing Folkestone, because she could accelerate, feeling the power of the car, after the stop start of the minor roads, then sweep off the motorway swinging down towards Cheriton. Slowing down at the lights meant, nearly there. Just by the lights, at the turnoff, there was a woman with her thumb out for a lift.

Ada said, "we're not in a rush, why not give her a lift?"

They did, she got in behind Ada, and said she hated that walk in the rain. As it was a glorious evening, Maeve glanced over to Ada, who was smiling and nodding. There was something odd about it all, nothing that Maeve could specifically put her finger on, more of a feeling. Going round by Folkestone West train station, Maeve turned to ask their passenger where she wanted to be dropped off, but as she had begun to expect, their passenger wasn't in fact in the car. She'd gone, disappeared, or had never been there.

"See, you are getting the hang of it." This seemed to cheer Ada up. "That lady often asks for a lift. She was killed by a car that didn't see her, and drove smack into her, but always appreciates it when someone stops for her. Lots of people can see her." Ada seemed to think that made it normal.

They dropped down to Sandgate. This had never been Maeve's home, but she had a feeling of home-coming. After Maeve's father died, Ada made the decision to move to the South Coast to be closer to Maeve and her granddaughters, luckily it was at the time when Sandgate was no longer fashionable, and before it was rediscovered. She had managed to buy a house on 'the Riviera', right on the seafront. It needed work doing to it, but it was an amazing location. The back garden opened directly onto the beach and fabulous sunsets over the sea. The house is worth a small fortune now, but Maeve didn't think that Ada would ever sell, because she had grown to love it.

They hadn't spoken for the last section of the journey. Maeve hadn't finished taking in the news that she had already communicated with spirits without being aware of it. Then, meeting the 'hitchhiker', had really thrown her. What would happen now? Clearly it wasn't a once off.

Ada was watching the thoughts pass across Maeve's face, and when she spoke it was in a voice that was sincere and serious.

"Look, I can't prepare you for what's going to happen next. Only you can do that. Know that I am here, call me, talk to me, I can help. You'll be fine, you are strong, but you don't have to go through this alone. It can be harrowing, or it can be trivial. It's all better if you share it, and I know how to keep a secret when need be." Maeve didn't answer, she wasn't ready.

The sun was going down as Maeve did her familiar, but ridiculously tight, three point turn in front of Ada's house. Maeve was conscious of Ada watching, she had never been that confident of Maeve's driving, and was always nervous that she might hit something. By the time Maeve stopped and turned to wave, Ada had already disappeared inside, she also didn't linger over goodbye's. Maeve headed up the hill back to Canterbury, home. She needed to take stock, she needed a refuge in the familiar. It was Saturday and part of the weekend ritual was pizza night, normally on a Friday, but

Orla didn't want to be that 'predictable', so the big change was to move it to Saturday, as it happened it worked out well. Maeve needed something predictable. She imagined that glass of red wine, with some jazz, Gregory Porter was her current favourite, in the background, and everything would be fine. Or so she thought.

CHAPTER 3

WHAT HAPPENED NEXT

Sunday morning started off perfectly. Another sunny day, the garden was alive with flowers, clematis scaling the hedge and merging into the hawthorn blossom. Wallflowers scenting the world. Up for her early cup of tea, listening to the morning birdsong Maeve was content. Even the cat, who Maeve thought was on the spectrum, now sitting in the middle of the floor under her feet, looked happy and content. Putting the experience of seeing spirits out of her mind, she opened the door onto the stone patio, and looking out at her garden, she was thinking of what vegetables she would focus on this year. Mangetout, peas and cherry tomatoes were the family favourites and those were in hand, maybe some of those small patty squash later in the summer? Or train some french beans up the posts? Still musing, and wondering if that was actually a nightingale in the garden, she went in for her shower.

They shared the family bathroom so timing and use of hot water had to be scheduled. Maeve didn't like to be under pressure and usually got up early to be the first one in, with enough time to luxuriate under the water.

This morning she wasn't focusing on the job in hand, and was already in the shower, when she remembered that she had left the fresh towel in the airing cupboard. Damn! The thought of a dripping walk, spoiled the pleasure of the hot water. It was Sunday, so not wanting to spoil the rest of day she minimised her internal grumbling, and pulled back the shower curtain. Surprisingly, there it was, still warm, sitting on the bathroom stool. Thinking that she was clearly losing the plot, and really needed a break as she was reaching out when she heard the "Ehmm".

It sounded like a man *in* the bathroom! She gasped, breathing in some water, and, as she was now choking, didn't manage a scream.

"I'm 'ere", he said.

It was a small bathroom, the shower-head was an attachment to the bath taps with a wall fixing, so standing in the bath, holding the shower curtain for protection, Maeve could see every nook and cranny in front of her.

"I'm here," he said again.

Continuing to wrap the shower curtain around her as she turned Maeve, now looked *in* the bath, this time she did scream. As she wasn't really a screamer, it sounded like the scream of someone who had turned the cold water on by mistake, and it wasn't likely to bring anyone running.

"Well at least I know you can see me now. It's taken long enough!"

She saw a man dressed-up in old fashioned livery with a white wig. It was as if he had stepped out of 'The Draughtsman's Contract' or maybe 'Barry Lyndon' or was going to a fancy dress party, but he was standing in the bath *with* her. Actually, his feet seemed to go through the bath and be standing on the floor. And he wasn't wet. Other than that, he was disturbingly real, and very close to her.

"Who the hell are you?", Maeve managed at last.

"I'm Edward Walker, man servant to Sir Edward Hales, at your service" he replied with a bow.

Maeve had so many questions, but the one that really bothered her was, had he seen her naked....? Not that with a semi-transparent plastic shower curtain around her, she was much better covered now. What she asked was,

"Why are you dressed-up like that?"

"It's the uniform that Sir Edward gave me. A bit poncy I thought, but he said 'versatile enough to work in the bed chamber, but also drive the coach as needed'. And to your other question, yes I can. That's a fine rump you have m'lady, and I don't mind sayin' it. Don't you worry yourself, I don't talk much."

This was to turn out to be completely untrue, Edward was a gossip, who talked incessantly to anyone and everyone, even if they couldn't hear, or see, him.

Edward explained he had 'a lot of pleasure' working at 'Hales Place' the Manor House, so he had stuck around….' His voice trailed off a bit here, Maeve wanted to know more, but right now her priority was to get dressed. Edward followed her closely and went on,

"I've 'watched over' the family since you came. I like to keep the place clean 'n' tidy, so I do a bit here 'n' there, some of the housework. Just to help out. I like to be useful."

He had decided that Orla was in his care, so she was the one he 'did for', and hence made her bed and tidied her clothes every morning.

This began to make sense to Maeve. Marianne liked order and neatness so her room was always reasonable. But since a small child, Orla, had spread herself everywhere, dirty clothes strewn all over the floor, books scattered, and clean clothes piled but never put away. However, since they had moved here, her bed was always made, and her clothes were tidied. Maeve had put this down to Orla starting to mature, now she knew otherwise.

Once over the shock of meeting Edward, and then warmly wrapped in the towel that he had laid out for her. Maeve had gone to get dressed, this time shoo-ing him from her bedroom with,

"I don't care if you are a spirit, you are not watching me get dressed!" She had decided not to mention any of this to the girls, for the moment.

With her film festival over, this was the first time in a

month that Maeve had the time to relax. Normally Sunday mornings were the sacred time of the week for Maeve and her daughters when they took the time to enjoy breakfast. They had the large cafetière of fresh ground coffee with plenty for a second cup, and the weekly treat of the 'fresh from the oven' perfect croissant or pain au chocolat.

This morning, Orla had seemed a bit on edge, and Marianne, a bit too quiet. They hadn't re-found their groove yet. Maeve wondered if each of them, in their own way, was putting on an act to be the perfect happy family, in the hope that that would make it true. She knew that they loved each other, but she felt that there were changes going on in all their lives that weren't being shared. She needed some time to deal with her own, so for the moment she felt helpless and unable to do anything about it.

After breakfast, trying to get her head straight, Maeve went for a walk to pick up the Sunday papers. If she was to accept the idea of 'spirits' being part of her world, how would it impact on her daily life? Apart from strange experiences, could one like Edward, discounting his uninhibited behaviour, actually be positive, even a help? Are they everywhere? Should she share this with the children? Would she have to? What if her children treated her the way she treated Ada, as someone 'a bit touched' craving attention? Maeve hadn't mentioned it so far because she hadn't worked through it herself yet, and up till yesterday, she had been a total skeptic.

Lost in her thoughts, she had forgotten to stop at the newsagent, and before she realised it, she was already halfway across Beverly Meadow heading towards the town centre. 'Typical', Maeve thought irritably, she often found that when not paying attention, her feet, or her car, would take her wherever her auto-pilot dictated.

"Hello", a pretty young Asian woman addressed her with some trepidation,"I don't want to bother you but…"

Here we go again, thought Maeve, she found the people who stop you and ask for money surprising, they don't always look in need. She kept a one pound coin in her pocket because she hated the look of disappointment if her pockets were empty. Holding out the coin, she began to wish the young woman good luck.

"No, no, I don't need money", she paused, "I think you're a friend, you have a kind face. Something bad is happening, I need your help. Please, go to the police, right now. Ask for one in particular, ask for Stephen Maguire. Tell him I sent you. You will hear more. When you can. You need to tell Stephen that I can talk to you."

She pointed to the city centre. Maeve turned back to ask her her name, but she was gone. Maeve didn't just see that the woman had gone, she sensed it too, she could no longer feel her presence.

Maeve found this disturbing, she looked like a lovely young woman, it was a sunny day, why would she give this meaningless message of foreboding? Maeve was aware that she didn't even have a name to reference. She had picked-up a profound sense of sadness, unlike with Edward where she felt first shock and then irritation, in himself, he seemed happy enough. This was very different, much darker. Was this some kind of test? And if it was, would it be the kind of test that she wanted to pass? On the other hand, she was also curious, who wouldn't be? Was there a puzzle to be solved? And this was her own experience, Ada wasn't involved at all yet, and depending on the outcome Maeve could keep it to herself.

Up till then she had been enjoying the walk. What harm if she was to walk to the police station and ask the question? If no one at the station knew a 'Stephen Maguire' then that would be that, end of, no harm done. Ada had been right Maeve thought, it was feeling the other person's upset that made her want to help. Normally the desire to fix people's problems was just for family, friends or work colleagues, but right now, she felt an overwhelming desire to help this woman out.

Maeve texted home to let them know that she was off for a walk and promised to drop into the Goods Shed on the way back. She would pick up some fresh sourdough bread, Ashmore cheddar, and some of Patrick's sausage rolls if he had any left, all that with enough fresh veg for a snack lunch and proper supper. These were all things that would go down well and if she was quick they would have time to do something nice in the afternoon too.

CHAPTER 4

SUNDAY, SUNDAY

Picking up her pace, she took the back route across Canterbury avoiding the tourists for at least half of the High St. Passing the Cathedral entrance in Buttermarket, she turned right via Pret and Castle St. She made it to the police station in about 30mins, not bad going.

As she approached the station, Maeve was conscious that she had never actually been inside the police station, or any police station for that matter. She had seen them in films and on TV, but didn't actually know if it was open, or how to get in? She stopped. This was one of those moments in life when you have to decide, it would be easy to turn around and go home, would she regret it? Given her decision to make life changes and having read any number of self-help books she knew that in order to change your life sometimes you have to say 'yes' and do things that make you uncomfortable. Maeve reflected on the many things in her life that she needed to change. This wasn't the obvious path, but what the hell? If she thought too much she might not do it, so without any further hesitation, she plucked up her courage, crossed the road, and headed toward the building. She found the entrance on Old Dover Road, walked up the ramp, and went in.

Sunday must be a quiet time at the station as there was no

one waiting, she went straight to the front desk. Conscious of the absurdity of her mission she half mumbled,

"is there a policeman called Stephen Maguire?", to the officer seated behind the desk.

As luck would have it, a tall man in a suit was passing on his way out for a break as she asked the question.

"I am Stephen Maguire. Who wants to know?" he said with a laugh, as he eyed her up, she was an attractive woman, definitely worth a second look.

Flustered, Maeve felt herself blushing, and stumbling over her words, she explained that she had met a girl in the park who had sent her to see him. He stopped.

"I have a very important meeting" pause, "with the best coffee in Canterbury!", he laughed at the thought that this was his 'important meeting'. "Why don't you walk with me and tell me what exactly happened. It sounds like it might be a prank. Someone playing a joke on you."

He wasn't unkind, Maeve thought, but clearly he also wasn't convinced, that she would tell him anything of value.

As they walked, Maeve retold her encounter. Thankfully, Stephen didn't think her mad and seemed to take her seriously, he asked very specific questions.

"Did this woman have a watch on, any remarkable jewellery? Or anything that might stand out as noticeable."

She told him all the details she could remember. By this time they had reached the coffee shop, and as he ordered the drinks, Steve quietly said

"I will tell you the whole story. Let's see if there is anyone outside in the back, it's often empty."

There were a few lone drinkers scattered at odd tables, none paying any attention to the newcomers. Once settled with excellent coffees in front of them he paused, as though to collect himself, and then began his side of the story.

"Nearly ten years ago now, not long after I started with the force, I was put on a murder case, a young Asian girl, a student in the University. One Saturday night, she was walking back to Uni after a few drinks with her friends in town. She took her normal route walking by the quieter back streets, as she crossed the park, Beverly Meadow, someone she knew attacked her and killed her, leaving her body in the bushes."

Maeve felt chills down her spine, and moved closer in.

"When I visited the crime scene the next morning, I felt something. It was almost as if she was still there, still alive, I couldn't talk to her, but I could feel her distress. I was also aware that she knew her attacker."

Stephen paused, his head down towards his cooling coffee with a slightly embarrassed look on his face, continued.

"Then I did a foolish thing, I mentioned it to my colleagues. Well, the lads in the station have seen a lot of the more unpleasant sides of life, and most are pretty hard nosed. 'Feeling something' was considered soft, and showed how green I was. It turned into a station joke, every time I appeared someone would go 'woohoo, the ghost is here to talk to you', or they would give me a message that the victim wanted to make a statement. I don't know why, but it really stuck, and I still get the occasional 'fake' message. When you started I thought someone had set you up to it. Looking at your face, it's more like we are both being set up."

There was nothing for it, Maeve thought, she had to tell him about her experience in Margate, about her mother, Ada, and what Ada does. Feeling exposed worrying that she would come across like one of the 'kooks' that hang onto Ada, the very ones she had spent her life avoiding, Maeve began with her disclaimer.

"To be very clear, this isn't something that I believe in! Well I didn't believe in, now I am not sure. You were the test for me."

She spoke quickly, then paused to collect her thoughts.

"The woman in the park was very specific about your name, but didn't give me hers. I thought if I went to the station, and they had never had a policeman by the name 'Stephen Maguire', that would be that."

Looking directly at Stephen she continued,

"the fact that you are a real person is a good thing, and yet, I don't really know what it means." Pause. " Earlier, you were asking me specific questions, why? And what was her name? She didn't give it to me."

He was quick to answer

"Susan Lin, not a very Asian name, but apparently a lot of people adopt an English name when they come over to study here. Makes it easier for us Brits to remember. Specific details are because I wanted to know if you had any information that wasn't already in the public domain. There are some details that we didn't share. We often get people from the same world as your mother, who make claims that they can communicate with the dead, normally for a fee. We try to fend them off so that they don't cause any further distress to the family."

"I know what you mean. That's exactly why I have never wanted anything to do with that world!"

She sighed, there was a pause in the conversation.

"It might be the coffee, but as we have been talking I have been replaying this morning's scenario in my mind, and there was one thing that I thought was a little odd and didn't think it was worth mentioning. But maybe it is. She, Susan, had only one earring. I know lots of people wear one as a fashion statement, but it wasn't like that. Both her ears were pierced, and as I said, her clothes were clean, neat, student style, probably Jack Wills, not cheap anyway. The earring was blue, like a sapphire stud, one of a pair, but the other one was missing. It didn't fit in with the rest of her to have only one. Another thing; I have been wondering, why did I immediately think she wanted money? I have this weird sense that her hands were dirty, I am not a hundred percent certain, but it's a strong impression. You know, the way they say you make a decision about someone within the first few seconds, whether you trust them, or find them attractive."

There was a beat, Steve was silent, he was looking at Maeve, she couldn't read him, was he looking at her because he found her attractive, or was it disbelief?

Emphatically Steve said, "You couldn't know that!"

His tone had changed completely. Maeve was taken aback

"Not know what?"

Stephen's body language had changed from that vulnerable moment of sharing, to professional, and highly irritated copper. Maeve was getting anxious, wondering what exactly, had just happened.

"I think this has gone far enough," he said, standing up to leave. "Someone from the station is definitely setting me up. What a shame, I thought you were a nice person. I liked your company. Too bad. They won't make a fool of me again."

Now annoyed at his lack of explanation, Maeve was equally sharp.

"Okay, I have no idea what you are talking about. Here is my number. When you have checked it out, you can call and apologise. If Susan contacts me again, and I have any further information, I will leave this message, 'coffee at the Micro Roastery', if you show up great, if not, then you don't."

She had done her bit, and had made the effort for the young woman. Almost to her surprise, he took it. Still cold, but calmer, he asked,

"What's your full name?"

"Maeve, Maeve McPhillips, I was pleased to meet you. Let's see shall we?" With that they both left, awkwardly walking in opposite directions.

That night, supper finished, Maeve had begun to recover her equilibrium. Her meeting with Steve ended up being more upsetting than meeting the woman in the park. Though she still couldn't shake off that sense of darkness and foreboding. Part of her thought, if she could just help this young woman, then she could shut it off, go back to normal, and not see any more spirits. So she still hadn't worked out what she would say to Marianne and Orla. The girls had gone off to their rooms to get ready for the morning. They had planned an episode or two of something light to watch on TV. She had half an hour to herself. She picked up the phone to Ada.

CHAPTER 5

STEVE'S STORY

Stephen Maguire, Steve to his friends, was 'one of the lads' at school. He had this really strong sense of fair play. He had been physically large and strong since a baby, as his mother frequently complained, he was a classic gentle giant. He was the one to settle any rows that got physical. No one took him on willingly, probably why joining the police force had been his ambition as far back as he could remember. Although popular he had never been part of a gang, he wasn't someone influenced by 'the general opinion', he liked to make up his own mind. It wasn't a problem, people left him alone, and he liked his own company.

Surprisingly, Steve stayed single. He had fallen in love with his childhood sweetheart, and back then, Steve thought he was set for life. There was no one else for him except for Angela. Angela, his angel, bright and sassy, she kept him in line. They had grown up together. She was the one who made sure he had the right kind of haircut, sharp jeans, comfortable loafers; she created a style that suited him, and they were a great pair. The two of them were making the best of long term plans, when she was killed in an accident. It was a young lad, drunk on a Saturday night, he took a corner too fast, by the time he saw her there was nothing he could do. The only vaguely positive thing anyone could say was that he was driving at such speed that Angela probably didn't feel a thing. Heartbroken, Steve buried himself in work after she died. He didn't want to feel that loss again in a hurry, however it would be eleven years ago this summer and he was also fed up with people feeling sorry for him. Maybe it was time to reconsider.

Steve often talked to himself. It seemed to help work things out. Maeve had intrigued him, and after he left her by the cafe, as he walked back to the station, he imagined telling her his backstory. Avoiding any mention of Angela of course, as he couldn't bear to see the pity it triggered in people's eyes.

He began going through the conversation in his head. 'Desert island discs' would be a cinch for me, I know the soundtrack of my life. I joined the police force straight from Uni, couldn't wait to get into uniform and do something I felt would make a difference.'

He could imagine the film playing in his head, the montage of getting the job, the uniform, and the gear, to the main theme for 'Top Gun' with Tom Cruise. Then shift of tempo, to being the newbie, the butt of the jokes, like being sent for 'a long stand', or the 'glass hammer', or the infantile 'funnel game' to wet your crotch. That part plays to 'What a difference a day makes', with the beautifully melodic Dinah Washington, as his ambitions slowly deflate.

A good 6'6, built to match, and not easily intimidated, at first he was impressed with everything. But the more he saw how out of date, and biased, some of the senior officers' views were, the more disillusioned he felt. He was let-down by people he thought were older and knew better. 'I mean everyone plays the occasional joke on people, but this is a serious job, and the senior management in my sector seemed to think it was okay. Okay to mock people.'

It was a signifier of the tone of the place. There were other attitudes that he had difficulty with. It was generally accepted that officers hated going to 'domestics', or domestic violence call outs, as if beating your partner was an acceptable part of marriage. Then the whole problem of police dealing with people with mental health issues. Internally the lads called them crazies or 'radio rentals' rhyming slang for 'mental' and made fun of them. These people needed medical, or social, care not the police. Steve found himself thinking, 'if this is how the police force works, how are we ever going to make the world a better place?'

With a little time he saw not all police are the same, and they were changing. But it was slow and internal rivalries meant no open discussions. For a young man when your idols come crashing down, and you realise that you are not Superman, you have to reassess your values. Steve decided the thing to do was to move on.

And move on he did, 'I stopped trying to change the world, and in return, found one of the greatest pleasures of my life. The freedom of riding a motorbike. To get out of the office I signed up for the Road Policing Unit, where you ride powerful motorbikes. I didn't know it beforehand, but once I got the hang of it, I loved it! Motorbikes are powerful, but elegant. The speed, the control and the ultimate sense of freedom.' He was back in the movie of his life and could imagine this montage to the BBC's soundtrack for F1, 'The Chain' by Fleetwood Mac with the insistent beat giving a tremendous feeling of excitement. 'I knew I was good and this was confirmed when I was put on the 'Bikesafe' initiative. This is a cracker of an initiative. We teach 'members of the public' meaning those who already ride motorbikes but do it dangerously, how to ride a bike properly. How to corner, how to maintain control in the wet, how to manage speed. It works really well to stop young men, (and it usually is young men), from killing themselves. I reckon we are the best motorbike riders in the world, I would say that wouldn't I? Actually, it's a life's ambition that I would like to prove. But I am getting ahead of myself, back to the beginning.'

Steve was getting his thoughts in order, a luxury you don't get when the person you are 'talking to' is actually there, facing you. In your head, things always come out right, and there are no misunderstandings. 'The first time that you do anything it sticks in the mind. Writing the first case notes, getting the paperwork done correctly, it’s as clear as day. Then in a flash, like no time has passed, it all becomes a blur of the mundane, and you are getting things done in time, done before your shift ends, or done before someone is chasing you for the info. No time to stop and think, just get it done. Then down to the pub for a few pints.’

Walking back to base, Steve had slowed his pace down as he re-lived it. ‘But the first time you see a dead body, the image never goes away.’ As he described the scene he was right back there in the moment. ‘I remember the morning being unusually quiet, stepping out of the traffic into the stillness of the park, the new growth turning everything that pale green, it's all crystal clear. There was no music, no backing track. Everything about that day is just like it was yesterday, hard to believe it’s nine years ago this month. I can hear the blackbird singing, which at the time seemed wrong, disrespectful to the young woman lying on the ground. Dumped, or rather rolled, into the long grass under the trees at the edge of the park. There had been enough time for dew to form on the spider's web. At first glance she could have been asleep with her back to us, one leg rolled over in the recovery position, but her head was at an awkward angle, twisted too far back. There was no look of surprise on her face. Probably why I thought she knew her killer. Her hands were dirty. I guessed that ‘he’ had pushed her onto her hands and knees, before he had broken her neck. I presumed a ‘he’, for the strength needed to move the body. Of course now I would say ‘assumption and presumption are the mother and father of all fuck-ups!’. Never assume anything, it's likely to lead you astray.

I hoped it had been quick for her sake, for ‘Susan’s’ sake. I used her name as soon as I knew it, out of respect for the dead.

On that morning, I felt like she was there with us, close behind me, leaning over my shoulder, looking down at her own body. I thought I saw her touching her right earlobe.

When I looked closer at the body, I could see that it was missing the right earring. It seemed important.

I was the junior on the case, my job was to listen, learn, take any notes that I was told to take, and get the tea. Not to come up with ideas. Not to interrupt the detective assessing what belonged to the crime scene, and what might have been added after the crime had been committed.

This feeling, that she was there, and trying to tell us, or tell me, something, was so strong, and the earring seemed so important to Susan, I stupidly opened my gob to the boss, the detective in charge. He was responsible for the Murder Book, my notes would be added to it later. Had I kept my mouth shut, or just brought it up as part of the process of gathering information, it would have been fine.

Too late. I had already blurted out that I had a feeling, I could sense the victim was still there with us, and that she was bothered by the missing earring. Well that was that. All the other pranks and jokes played on the newbie up to this point paled into insignificance. I became the 'ghost seer'. It got so bad I thought it affected the way we managed the investigation. We never did find the missing earring, I thought it was significant, but this time kept my trap shut.

Equally, when the press release was being written the earring was one of the key facts that we held back, to use as a test for any self declared eye witnesses, or friends, who were out with her that night. You need that because murder cases often attract the wrong sort of people, the curious, the amateur detectives, the cranks, and the charlatans, we take statements from them all. At this stage of the investigation, you just don't know what's going to be a dead end, and what's going to be the critical piece of information.

Now, nine years later, how could a random woman know about the earring?'

CHAPTER 6

THE FIRST TIME

Canterbury has changed considerably over the last ten years, it is much more cosmopolitan now. When I have the time, I like to wander the streets, and breathe in the passers-by. Absorbing their exoticness, listening to snatches of throw away conversations. Go for a coffee, or a glass of something seasonal, and reflect on life.

I don't pick a theme to dwell on, often it's from something overheard. Today, some indiscreet words floated my direction that took me back to my first adventure. How do you know who you are? When do you realise the defining characteristics that make you special?

Susan, that young Asian girl was my defining moment, not that it is something I can share. I wanted to tell my mother. I wanted to ask her, was it her coldness towards me as a child, or was I born like this, special. The girl was a beautiful young woman, and that Saturday evening she just walked passed me, didn't pay me any attention. No respect. She knew who I was. I wanted to get closer to her, to touch that unblemished smooth skin.

As she walked passed me I changed direction, backtracking, walked a little faster and closed in behind her. She turned, the suddenness of her movement almost landed her head directly into my hands. As if she was a gift, I knew exactly what to do, like I had been taught the movement. A quick, sharp twist of the head, the neck clicked, she went limp. I suppose it was the speed of it all that made me drop her, she fell over onto her hands and knees.

I felt nothing. It was the lack of upset, or disgust, at this dead body that was vaguely surprising. I didn't pause to think at the time, it was later, that I took the time to reflect. In the moment I felt intense calmness, at peace with myself. That is when I discovered that I liked it.

CHAPTER 7

ANOTHER BODY

Ada and Maeve talked on the phone, and agreed to meet the next day. Their relationship had begun to change. They were beginning to work things out. It needed a lot of going back over the past, seeing things from different perspectives. Legacies of blame and disappointment hung between them, but there was a new sense of urgency to get through this, and maybe arrive at a place where they could be on the same side. Right now, it was still a bit like walking on eggshells.

They met in Folkestone, neutral ground. 'The Chambers' cafe/bar in Cheriton Place, a flat white and a latte. They had ordered enough to take the corner table, and buy the time to go through it all again. Not many people were in at this time of day, so no one was going to rush them.

Ada started.

"I am hearing things too. I don't mean I am hearing things, I mean people, spirits, are talking to me too."

Dramatic pause, Maeve had no time for the 'drama' of it all.

"Well don't leave it there…what are they saying to you?"

Ada continued, "Sorry, I am so used to people needing to feel that sense of mystery, needing the occult to come with incense and deep sighs. It's part of me now, I am trying to get this right for you, so be a little patient with me. What I'm hearing is that something bad is happening. Someone evil, is doing something bad. I know it sounds vague and portentous all the stuff you hate, love, but that's all I've got at the moment. Oh, and they like you, the spirits like you. I guess that means that you will hear more from 'Susan', or from others. God love 'em, whoever they are, they trust you."

Maeve frowned, "does that mean that you have a spirit, like a 'familiar', who's a voice for other spirits, or does one spirit keep contacting you until their issue has been resolved?"

Ada smiled, "that depends on them, and on you. It only becomes clear when you look back on things. In my professional opinion.."

Maeve winced at the idea that this was a profession.

"..in my professional opinion, you'll have to wait and see." Ada leaned back, and closed her eyes, "I am feeling urgency and upset, so maybe not long."

Maeve wasn't ready to share her experience with Edward, why make things more complicated than they already were? If she could resolve Susan's issue, she could stop there. Maeve was glad the bar was empty and no one could overhear the conversation. It wasn't quite warm enough to sit outside today, but the cafe was at a crossroads of shopping streets, and through the large windows they could see people coming and going. Maeve found the ordinariness of people shopping, friends stopping to chat, and going about their everyday business, comforting.

Later, she left Ada to do her own shopping. She was considering if she really wanted to be a part of this weird world, as she wandered back to her secret parking space, at the back of the church. She was at a change point in her life, she'd finished her contract, and wasn't sure what to do next. Time for a career change, or just take whatever event came up to pay the bills? She had enough savings for six months, and had wanted to take some time off to think, even before the dramas of the last few days.

She drove out via Cheriton, and on her way, wanting a moment of peace to reflect, she turned into the Enterprise park, right before the M20 roundabout. She had worked here some years ago when it was just built. It was familiar, it had changed since she was there, but still had the same feeling, a bit soulless, not much character. There were a lot more buildings now, but you could still see the railway tracks. She had a short stroll around, but felt like she didn't belong anymore and had no business being there. She was disappointed that the past didn't provide any answers, and yet she knew that when the time was right, she would know what to do, it simply wasn't today.

She got back into the car, started it up, turning to leave, she stopped for a moment to take a last look just as a young man bundled himself into the passenger seat. Shocked, she sat there, not sure what to do.

Finding her voice, she tried to sound confident with a firm "What do you want?"

He didn't look at her, he had a denim jacket over a black hoodie which was half up, covering most of his face.

"We don't have much time, I have much to tell you, let's go!"

He didn't seem threatening, just in a hurry.

Maeve registered exactly where they were, the track she could see in the distance is the first place the EuroTunnel freight trains slow down coming over from France. She had seen people creeping from under train carriages years ago.

Maeve tried again, slowly,

"Are you seeking asylum here? I am not the right person for you to talk to. You need a policeman, or a customs official."

He was impatient,

"No, I have papers. I need to talk to you. I believe that you are a friend. We must drive, so I can talk to you."

His English was good enough, but clearly not a local.

The word 'friend' triggered her memory and the penny dropped, he might be the next spirit to contact her. Beginning to see how these things worked, Maeve went with the flow, started to drive and decided to head home, fewer decisions to make, and if change was needed something would happen. As the car moved off, he started to talk.

"My name is Kamal Ghazi. I have information for you, and then please contact my mother in Iraq."

Not wanting to interrupt Maeve waited.

"I am not long gone. I have papers in my bag. My bag is hidden by the bushes near the road. I show you where. I have business I want your help with. Then you can find my mother's address. You can call her, tell her I didn't make it. I tried but I couldn't tell anyone. Now I will tell you."

Maeve really wanted to stop, and get a notebook to write this down.

"No, no time, you can remember."

Clearly Kamal could read her thoughts too. She was desperate to have a good look at him. And she was worried about having to remember everything he said as she was driving. So first she focused on listening, and was driving slowly.

"I am Kurdish. I am a student in University of Kent, studying rockets, full name 'Rocketry and Human Spaceflight'. There are other students in the Uni from Iraq, they are learning how to make chemical weapons to use against Western forces in our region. These people are bad people, not my people, they would like to kill me, but everyone thinks we are the same because we come from the same country. This is not true. I tried to tell the officials. I love the UK, but many, many people in the UK think we are all 'bloody foreigners', and if you look Arab like me, and have a bag, then you are a 'terrorist' or 'suicide bomber'. So no-one would listen. Then my visa was taken away. Same thing happened to many students, they said I paid for my exam results, my English was not good enough, I was sent home."

By this time they had got through Hawkinge and were on

a relatively quiet, straight stretch of road. Maeve could see his body without turning much, she twisted to see his face. Dark hair, brown eyes, olive skin with clearly defined features he was a handsome young man. Calm, but when he spoke it was with energy and passion. His clothes had some mud on them, and the knees of the jeans had rips, could be fashion, or could be that they were worn out. She didn't stare because she didn't want to take her eyes off the road for too long.

Aware of the pause in his story she asked,

"Did these other Iraqis…?"

Her question trailed off, as she was not sure if she could address the fact that he was a spirit directly or not.

"No, no, they don't know that I hate them. They are Iraqis, I am a Kurd from Iraq, I want them in prison, but they don't know that, they think I don't fight, I am not a real man like them. Why does the University not look into their reason for coming here? They are fanatics, and they have to be stopped! They are very bad for my people. Sure they hate the Americans, and the British, but also they want to kill, to exterminate, all the Iraqi Kurds too!"

Another pause, Kamal was lost in thought.

Suddenly, he seemed to realise that time was passing.

"I have to tell you how I got here. I got a new visa, and came back to finish my studies, but on my journey I made a mistake, and got off the train in Folkestone. I should have stayed on till Ashford and changed there. It was late. I thought, quicker to take a taxi. There were no taxis. But a car and the driver said 'where to?' I told them, and £35 was a good price, so I took the car."

He stopped for another moment, it was all very raw, he was still processing it.

"We passed a village near here. Up a hill where the trees made a tunnel overhead. On till there was a driving entrance to something off the road, the driver said that he had to stop to use the bathroom. 'Get out and stretch your legs.' I opened the car door. Habit made me take my bag with papers."

By now, Maeve had guessed exactly, where the driver had

stopped. It was at the entrance to Barham Crematorium. She thought that whatever happened, it had happened there, and it was ironic, to die outside a crematorium. So far, Maeve had been listening intently, whilst still managing to concentrate on driving through the village.

"I took a few steps, looked around. Then the car engine was going fast, the driver hit me with the car. My bag went out of my hands, into the bushes, by the tall tree. The driver didn't stop. He drove the car over and back. Until I stopped."

Silence.

On up the hill, she drove under where the branches of the trees had indeed grown over the road intertwining to form a green tunnel, at last, she pulled into the entrance to the crematorium with its own mini roundabout, and stopped the car. Of course, when she turned to look directly at Kamal, he was no longer in the car.

So many things went racing through her mind. Too much, and too little, information. He wanted her to find his papers. Then she could contact his mother. Those seemed to be the most immediate tasks. He had thrown, or flung, his bag into bushes by the tall tree.

If she started rummaging, would that damage the crime scene? Just then, a number of cars began to leave the crematorium car park, all going round the mini roundabout, and driving past the spot she had guessed was the crime scene. If there had been any evidence on the road, there wasn't any more. She got out of the car, and walked across the driveway towards the biggest tree. It was a large evergreen. Looking around where the base of the tree was closest to the hedge, there, in the middle of the neatly trimmed hedge, she spotted a small shoulder bag. The kind people use for travel documents. It was wedged in the hedge, almost as if someone had posted it there. The brown leather blended with the mature branches of the shrubs making it almost invisible. She reached in, and pulled it out, the bag was worn, either well used, or had been there for some time.

Looking down, she noticed that there were tyre tracks on

the grass verge, similar to the ones she would probably leave on the other side. Was this evidence? Or just the last car who stopped here. She felt totally ill equipped to deal with any of this. Sod it, she thought, taking the bag back to her car. She needed to know if this was even relevant. Sitting inside she opened it. There was an Iraqi passport. The text was in Arabic, luckily the name was also in English, Kamal Ghazi!

What next?

CHAPTER 8

A WHOLE NEW WORLD

Maeve got home and phoned Ada. Who else could she turn to? But then again, having disparaged Ada's world for so long, asking for help wasn't necessarily easy for Maeve. Ada listened,

"You've jumped right in at the deep end, haven't you?", she sniffed.

Ada always enjoyed being the centre of attention, having Maeve enter her world was great, giving them something to share, but rivalries can be innate, and this was definitely Ada's turf. Maeve did sense a little tension, might Ada be irritated that she wasn't the one at centre of all this drama? All of this was whirring through Maeve's head, but there was no time for that, this was urgent.

"But what do I do now?" Maeve knew she sounded a bit pathetic, and 'whingey'.

Ada could trigger responses in Maeve, that Maeve had spent a considerable amount of time and money in therapy, trying to stop. One of these was sounding 'whingey'. It didn't bode well for developing this new, and better, relationship.

Ada, "well, you are the one he chose to appear to, I go that way every time I come over to Canterbury, and I haven't seen him. I suppose you do what he asked you to? Sorry love, have to dash. Talk to you tomorrow." With that the phone went dead.

Great.

Maeve was now in possession of potentially vital evidence, and she felt completely on her own. Think. What are you supposed to do in a situation like this? Racking her brain for anything useful, she worked through options. She couldn't think of any friends who might have a clue. The books she'd read were fiction, so not reliable. She'd seen the occasional bit from Crimewatch on TV, and seemed to remember each episode ended with the Crimewatch phone number. This wasn't on TV, so no number......Whichever angle she considered, it looked more, and more, like making contact with Steve was the right next step.

"Oh God!" This is not what she wanted to do. In fact, he was probably the last person she wanted to speak to. He hadn't been back in touch, so must think that, at best, she was a flake, 'not all there', or at worst, trying to make money out of those left behind. Not quite an ambulance chaser for the injured, more of a hearse chaser for the bereaved. Not a pleasant image. Best not to overthink it, or she would convince herself to tell him to get lost before she had even asked the question. Taking a metaphorical deep breath. She called the station and left a message for Steve. 'Coffee in the Micro Roastery? Maeve', and she left her number.

As she put down the phone, she stopped for a moment. Up to now, she had been so busy trying to figure out the next practical step, that she had forgotten to check-in with herself. Was she okay? She had been sitting at the kitchen table, which often stood in for an office desk. She looked down, and noticed that her hands were shaking. Time for a cup of tea, she didn't like sugar in her tea, but it's the thing they give you when you've had a shock, isn't it? She'd have a Rich Tea biscuit instead, and got out a pen and some paper. Better to make notes, make it something with a list to be dealt with, have items to cross off. Don't freak out.

The bag was sitting in the middle of the table in front of

her, in the middle of the uncleared breakfast debris. The jar of marmalade, the butter, and remaining dirty side plates. The table was covered with a William Morris design piece of waxed cloth, from Liberty's, it had been there for years, but she was focusing on it as if she had never noticed it before. She really wasn't okay. As she moved, it was as if waking up from a daze, and she got up suddenly. Seeking some level of normality, she started clearing the table, and making the tea. This was routine, and that was good.

By the time she sat down, at the now clean table, mug in hand, things were a little better. 'Focus on something', she told herself. 'The list. The list needed to be divided into sections. Facts known; Facts that can be checked; Things to do in order of importance. Write out the things we know, suspect, or need to confirm.' Giving herself logistical problems to solve, was grounding. She wrote as much as she could from what she remembered, and left blanks for the bits to be filled in. The bit that stood out was his mother's name and contact info, if there was any. She began to rethink the journey, Kamal had seemed solid, real. At the same time she had begun to doubt herself, 'was he actually dead? If he was, who would know? The hospital?'

She was about to make the call, when the phone rang, an assistant had a message from Steve, 'Out of the station this afternoon, tomorrow morning 10am okay for you?' She told them it was, relieved that she could put off having to speak directly to him, even if only till tomorrow morning.

Maeve hadn't opened the bag since that first confirmatory look. She still had a feeling that it needed someone official to do it, so that they would do the right thing. Even as she thought this, it seemed faintly ridiculous. She didn't even know if a crime had been committed for real. Still, she couldn't bring herself to go through his things.

She had some time before the girls got in from school, so decided to call the hospital and find out. Knowing one thing for sure would help. She was automatically put on hold, and as she listened to a 'tinny' version of Vivaldi, Maeve reflected that she didn't even know *when* the 'accident' had happened. The woman who answered may have meant well, but was definitely not helpful, she trotted out some stock phrases, "we are not in a position to give out that kind of information, in situations like this the next of kin are notified," as she was talking another call came through " ...please hold,...." While Maeve waited, she thought about his mother, so far away, not knowing, and then she began to think what it would be like for her, if that had been one of her daughters .....she hung up, put her head in her hands, and cried.

Maeve limped through the rest of the evening. Supper was a pretty silent affair. Both Marianne and Orla were preoccupied, neither wanting to talk, and each responded to the standard 'how was your day?' monosyllabically. With no one in the mood to talk, they went back up to their rooms as soon as they had finished eating. Maeve knew that she should tease out their issues, but at this stage, she was emotionally drained and functioning on auto-pilot.

Now that she could see Edward, she noticed that he was doing some of the tidying up that she had previously given the girls credit for. This was another thing that needed to be dealt with when she had the energy, they needed to be part of a team, all pulling together. Seeing him brought her right back to the big question, what did she want to do about this 'seeing spirits'? She was exhausted, and her mind was blank, full of cotton wool, and as she couldn't even penetrate her own thoughts, she was never going to come to any conclusions. Tomorrow, she thought, tomorrow I'll wake up fresh and ready to work all of this out. So she poured herself another glass of wine, and went to watch some comfort food television.

CHAPTER 9

REALLY?

The walk into town, the next morning, was everything Maeve had hoped for. She took a slightly longer route, aiming to avoid any spirits, and picked up a bracing pace to help marshal her thoughts. Turning forty was the milestone that had pushed her to reassess her life. Seeing spirits had never been a part of her game plan. If Ada was right, then this was an ability, or a gift, that at some point she had chosen to reject. Which meant that it was possible that she could reject it again. This gave her some comfort, at least in her mind she had regained a sense of control. She wanted to help Susan, and if it really was a gift, then wouldn't it be a good idea to see how it worked before turning her back on it?

Maeve didn't want to feel embarrassed over who would pay for the coffee, so she had got to the cafe early. She was sitting, in the most discreet spot in the corner, nursing her favourite, a flat white. Most of the other customers were in for their morning take-away, so the tables were pretty empty.

She had begun to deal with her relationship with Ada, true it wasn't all going to plan, but she had made a start. What about her children? Who really weren't children any more.

Marianne, with whom during that last year she had done the rounds of universities. She had her heart set on

Cambridge. Maeve was thinking that Marianne had the brains, and she worked hard, she should be fine. At the same time Maeve hated the pressure it put on her, and was worried about how Marianne would handle it, if she didn't get the grades she needed. In fact Maeve hated the whole system from GCSE to A level. In her view the kids didn't get a break, the pressure never let up, and all this at a time in their life when hormones were raging, and they were finding out who they really were. It's tough. She worried that Marianne kept it all bottled up inside, and might have a breakdown before the exams even arrived. Maeve had suggested that she take a break, and on one of the long weekends go away somewhere, maybe see her Dad, but that had been met with a snort of 'you really don't understand do you'. She had clearly hit a nerve, definitely a sign of stress.

Orla was dealing with the imminent GCSEs, and she seemed to be without a bother for the moment, taking it all in her stride, which in itself was cause for concern. Orla did most of the table banging about world politics. Maeve had noticed her change in clothes, which were definitely moving towards the hippy look, not suited to school uniform. Maeve hoped that this wasn't developing into a real issue; she hadn't yet had that talk, about tattoos being something you might regret later in life, but felt it was coming. She was wondering if she took Orla shopping would that help or would that be the worst thing ever, when a shadow fell across the table.

Looking up Maeve saw Steve, coffee in hand. He looked a little sheepish.

"Sorry about yesterday," he said as he sat down opposite her.

Somehow this seemed to embolden her,

"So you bloody well should be! What made you change like that?"

Steve didn't answer immediately, he added two scoops of sugar to his coffee, and stirred it slowly,

"You said something you couldn't have known unless you read the files."

"Or unless someone I met told me!", Maeve still had a sharpness in her tone.

Steve came back with,

"How likely do you think that is? I mean, would you believe it if a random stranger came looking for you, and told you a ghost wanted to talk to you? To be fair, I take that back, given your recent experience, you probably would. Anyway, I ascertained that you were not set up by any of my colleagues, which is a step in the right direction. So I apologise. I hope that you accept my apology?" Steve wasn't making fun of her, but still there was a lightness in his voice which she liked.

Maeve wanted to be witty and intelligent, but the best she could manage was

"Apology accepted. Let's start again, shall we?"

Pause. Steve smiled assent.

Then she went on,

"I wanted to meet you this morning, because I have something that could be more important."

Maeve started recounting her trip back from Folkestone, retelling Kamal's story and ending up with the bag.

"I don't know anything about how the police work, so I may have spoiled evidence, but then again, I still don't really know if he was killed."

She sounded more vulnerable now, as she went on,

"I tried calling the hospital to see if he was there, but no joy. At Barham, I did open the bag, and took out a passport. As soon as I saw his name in the passport, I put it straight back in the bag and shut it. I was shocked that I was touching something that had belonged to him directly. I didn't know what to do, I thought we might go through it together? What do you think?"

Steve took a deep breath,

"not sure where to start. First, if this was evidence then your fingerprints and DNA would be all over it, so you would be the prime suspect, and I would be reading you your rights before taking you down to the station."

Maeve turned white.

"Don't worry. That's not going to happen. It's okay, really." He put his hand over hers, to reassure her. It was warm and comforting, she felt better, and recovered her colour. He continued,

"No bodies, or even serious accidents, have been reported anywhere near there in years."

Pause, as Steve went back through his mind for any old cases that might fit.

"Actually thinking about it, there was a guy killed in a hit and run accident some years back at Barham. When people take the wrong exit off the motorway, sometimes they turn round at the crematorium. It must have been dark and the driver didn't see the victim, we assumed the victim had been hiding in the bushes, and stepped out at exactly the wrong time. He had no papers and looked foreign. Driver probably panicked, and certainly didn't leave enough evidence for us to identify them. Then no one came forward looking for a missing person, no one to identify the body. We get a lot of asylum seekers in East Kent, from the ferries, or EuroTunnel. No papers, no ID, no money; conclusion, probably an unlucky asylum seeker."

Maeve started to frown,

"But what if I am right? That would make it murder, wouldn't it? Okay, the timing might be wrong. Kamal, the victim, the spirit, may think it has just happened, and maybe it was a few years back. This bag has all the information in it. And his photo is in his passport. Do you keep photo records of dead people? If he was a student at UKC, then the University would have a record of him, wouldn't they? We could check it out."

This was a new direction. It would mean more work for Steve, he had enough to do without digging up old cases, but still it shouldn't be too much just to prove Maeve wrong. If she was right however, that would be a whole different kettle of fish, and he wasn't ready to go there yet. Maeve on the other hand, felt confident, there were practical things she could do, and now she had someone in the real world to talk it over with.

Steve still had his hand over hers in friendly reassurance, when Maeve felt someone staring at her. She turned her head and gave an involuntary exclamation

"Shit!".

Orla was standing in the cafe staring at her and Steve. Maeve panicked, there were so many things wrong with this which she wasn't ready to explain. Orla turned and left. Maeve pulled her hands away embarrassed.

"Steve, I can't talk anymore. Can you dig around at your end and I will check in with the University? See you here, same time tomorrow?"

Without waiting for an answer, she grabbed her bag, leaving Kamal's behind, and almost ran out of the cafe, to chase after Orla.

Steve, finding himself suddenly alone, was part-surprised, and part-amused, wondering what had just happened. Whenever he could, he was a regular in the cafe at this time of day, so it shouldn't be an issue. He would just have to wait till tomorrow to find out. He had some time this afternoon, and could check the files, he wanted to show Maeve what a good investigator could do, or maybe, he just wanted to impress her with what *he* could do. As he collected up his stuff, in his mind he was playing the tense music from the trailer of 'Knives Out' with Danial Craig, what was it called? Oh yes,'Play the Ponies' by Jo Blankenburg, great track.

Gathering her thoughts as she did a fast walk, Maeve rounded the corner. She could see Orla, striding ahead of her along the High Street. First Maeve thought, why wasn't she in school? What the hell is going on! Orla had never done anything like this before. Or had Maeve just not known what she has been up to? Back in the cafe, Maeve had only had a quick look at Orla, but she could have sworn she had glimpsed a tattoo on her neck, and she had certainly seen a nose ring. Could she have got all that done this morning? Maybe she had been concerned about the wrong daughter.

Catching up with Orla, she called out in her most severe tone,

"Stop! Young lady, we have to talk, now. Right now!" Orla was in serious trouble.

Orla froze, standing stock still, until Maeve caught up with her.

Without waiting for her mother to say anything else, Orla, fists clenched by her side, launched into a tirade,

"How dare you! How dare you say anything to me, when you are sneaking off to meet some man! Does Marianne know about this? Does Dad? Am I the last one to hear? Mum, do you even care about us?"

Maeve was stunned, completely shocked. She had been preparing to be the outraged mother. This was her daughter, this was her little girl, that she kissed better when she fell over, that she loved. But it didn't sound like her at all. The shock, was like a slap in the face, and made her stop, stand still, and breathe.

Maeve had to do a double quick reassessment, and get her own emotions under control. Inside she knew that this was the time for her to be the 'grown-up', that this wasn't the time for her own outrage, and that Orla's outburst was likely to be a defensive attack. It wasn't easy. The thought she clung to, was that no matter what was happening, she loved her daughter, and had to do whatever it took to make it right.

As soon as she had somewhat cooled down, Maeve reached out, not knowing how this would be received, but knowing she had to take the risk anyway. She put her arms around Orla, giving her an all-enveloping hug. Orla was rigid for a few minutes, and then, just melted. Pulling back to take a look at her, Maeve saw tears running down Orla's face, Maeve realised that she too was crying. They stood there for a moment in silence, looking at each other.

Maeve spoke softly,

"Love, whatever it is, whatever happens to you, or to me, we can always sort it out if we talk to each other. I'm sorry, so sorry. I have things that I should have told you, but seeing a new man isn't one of them! Clearly you have things to tell me too!"

Orla wasn't ready to forgive Maeve, and was still verging on hysterical,

"...all you do is stuff for the festival, you haven't had time for us! You have no idea what's really going on. There's lots you don't know." Orla was sobbing.

Maeve put her arms around her again, more hugs and tears. Maeve had been right when she felt that Orla was on edge. Now she needed to face it directly. Shouting wasn't the best way to deal with things, now the best thing was to get Orla to calm down a bit.

"I know you love your Dad, and we need to talk about it. I know that I avoid it. And we will do when we are all together. But that's not the real problem, is it? I mean you aren't in school, and unless I'm blind, that's a nose piercing! All of which happened before you saw me in the cafe."

Tense silence from Orla.

Maeve wanted to diffuse the situation, she smiled as she asked,

"How do you blow your nose? Do you have to take the ring out?" Then they found they were both laughing as Orla hiccuped, and tissues were found to blow noses, and wipe the tears.

Now that the emotional level was coming down to normal, and that things were out in the open, they could move to some proper talking. Maeve was back in control, thinking that she had been facing more emotional trauma in the last few days, than she had in the last ten years. Food in a warm cafe would help.

"Let's not stay on the High Street! How about we go for a hot chocolate in the Café St. Pierre?"

CHAPTER 10

WHY DIDN'T I SEE THAT BEFORE?

They had missed the morning rush of customers, and got the table that looked out on the baskets of flowers hanging along the brick wall of the back terrace. Pain au chocolat, mocha, and hot chocolate, they might suffer from a sugar overload but some days you just need to do that.

Still moving from laughing to crying, Maeve and Orla began to share, and establish a new bond based on who Orla was becoming. It was true that Maeve had been absent for some time with the festival, and before that, had focused on Marianne, trying to be there for her. Fitting in all the 'open day's' they went to, around her work, hadn't been easy. Orla had seemed happy enough, never stressed about schoolwork, and always ready to share her opinions about world wrongs that needed to be righted, so Maeve hadn't set aside any special one-on-one time with her. It seemed like today, it had all rolled into one, and rather than strung out over many reasonable discussions, it had turned into Orla's bombshell.

"Mum, I don't want to finish school. I want to save the world." Maeve was about to say something when Orla stopped her and asked not to be interrupted, "I want to tell you everything, I have thought about it and I don't want you to stop me!"

Maeve knew that this was a pivotal moment in their relationship, and listening was what she had to do.

"Go on love, I won't say a thing till you are ready."

Orla took a deep breath,

"basically your generation has fucked the planet, I said 'fucked', not to shock you, but because I can't find another word for it. I don't have a future if the world is going to end. I have been following Greta Thunberg, and she is 100% right. Climate change is the wrong word, it sounds too mild, our whole way of life is about to be destroyed, and we are doing nothing!"

The passion was driving Orla on, she was articulate and compelling. Clearly this was where she had been putting her effort, rather than schoolwork.

"I know at home we talk about it, but then you shrug, with a 'what difference does one small family make' attitude. And apart from recycling, and using a bamboo toothbrush, what do we do about it?"

With a sigh, that seemed beyond her age, she went on,

"We have run out of time, we have to act now. I can't see the point in school, or university, if there is no future for me to be a part of! Greta Thunberg, was younger than me when she started protesting, see the difference she has made. My life is a complete waste, I'm 16 and I have done nothing!"

Maeve felt sad, that Orla was so frustrated. In times past she would have tried to cheer her up, chivvy her along, but that ship had sailed. She was listening to a committed, reasoned young woman. A beat. Orla resumed,

"So I want to be an Eco Warrior, I want to protest, sit outside parliament, and hug trees." In a final flourish she ended with "I want to do whatever it takes, until I can see a future for my generation."

Silence.

Maeve was taking it all in, of course she knew that basically, Orla was right, but she had never faced the direct, and in fact very logical, implication of it. It's a good question, what is the point in going to school when everything you know might disappear overnight. Floods, massive storms, a tornado in England, an earthquake in Kent, all these things had been unthinkable, and then they had actually happened. Close to home, right here. What if Orla was the one, making the right decisions?

Maeve was also thinking about the spirits who had found her. Susan, and Kamal, both of them were students who Maeve imagined had worked hard, but who never got to have the choices that their education should have given them. Sometimes life is cruel. Sometimes life is short.

"Mum? You okay? You can talk now." It had clearly taken a lot out of Orla, she looked deflated.

Maeve moved around and gave her another long hug and rubbed her back.

"I don't really know what to say, or even to think, except that you do have a really good point. This doesn't mean I agree with you completely, I am just thinking aloud here." Maeve didn't want to get herself into a situation where she found herself agreeing to something she hadn't had the time to consider properly.

"All of my experience would say, finish school, get a good degree, then you will have choices."

She paused, thinking again about those spirits, and about life choices that she hadn't made, or rather, things she had done because they were 'normal', and the times when she had just drifted. She wasn't as passionate, or maybe not as brave, as Orla.

"My world has been turned upside down over the last few days. Now, I am thinking that perhaps 'carpe diem', seize the day, or do what you have to do, while you still can, might be a better way to deal with life. So I don't know if it's crazy, or absolutely the right thing to do." Quickly adding,

"I haven't agreed to anything. What I am saying, is, let's think very seriously about it."

Orla, still red eyed, was beaming,

"Phew! Mum, at least you are not saying an outright no.

That's something. And I didn't expect you to be so reasonable, I was ready for a fight."

Orla had returned to being the teenager Maeve had seen at breakfast. It was something that Maeve had noticed before, this ability to shift from child to adult as if inhabiting the adult body for too long was wearing.

Relaxing into her younger self, Orla went on,

"I am super glad we are talking and you aren't freaking out. I feel much better."

The atmosphere had changed, emotions spent, and with a sugar fuelled return to semi-equilibrium they sat in silence for a minute or two.

As if she hadn't taken a break, Orla resumed,

"...two other things. First, I don't want to go clothes shopping with you, just in case you were thinking of it. No more new clothes. We don't do 'new', when there are plenty of old things we can reuse. Reduce, Reuse, Recycle, you are going to get tired of hearing me say that. No more unnecessary waste. Also, no more meat! I'll let you take some time to get used to that, but I'm not eating any more meat."

Maeve knew that today was the beginning of a lot more sharing with Orla, and Marianne. Like Maeve, Orla wanted to get back to a level of normality between them, so with only a short pause, to let that sink in she continued,

"Also, Ada said I was to wait till you told me first, but you haven't so I'm not waiting anymore. I can see dead people too. Mostly I see children and teenagers. I'm not like Ada, I don't go looking for them, they find me."

Maeve made an involuntary intake of breath, almost a gasp, as she put her hand over her mouth. Orla had known this for years, so had added this latest bombshell as though it was nothing.

"I've always known I could see people who others couldn't, but years ago when I tried talking to you, you didn't seem to understand me, but Ada did."

Orla didn't mean this as a dig at Maeve, more as a statement of fact, but it hurt Maeve to realise that her own issues had caused her to dismiss Orla when something was this important. Orla carried on,

"When I was small, Ada treated it as if it was normal, and said I was to talk to her about it. As I got older she said best not say anything to you until you stopped being in 'denial'. At the weekend she mentioned something about it, but you know what she's like, Ada loves the mystery and drama of it all so didn't say what exactly had happened only that you'd probably tell me in your own time. As we are sharing...Is now a good time?"

"Oh my God!" Leaving school, and now this. It was too much for Maeve, who thought she had managed pretty well 'till now, didn't say anything else for a good few minutes, just shook her head and repeated,

"Oh my God!". At one point she wondered if she had inadvertently stepped into a Christopher Nolan movie like 'Memento', and that none of this was actually real!

Orla could see that Maeve was struggling, so tried to give her some space by talking to fill in the silences,

"Ada says it runs in the family, and we have a great-great something in Northern Ireland, who was burned for being a witch. I'm not sure that's even relevant, but it all adds to the colour of the story." There was something about the way that Orla had taken this in her stride that calmed Maeve down. When she felt that she had given Maeve enough time, Orla changed the subject,

" Since when did you 'hold hands' with, some guy? I think it's time for you to share."

Maeve, still reeling from the series of revelations, managed to mumble her way through her side of the last few days. The lady in Margate, Susan and Kamal, all repeated but Maeve didn't mention Edward, if Orla hadn't seen him maybe it would be better not to say anything.

"Must be a bit of a shock for you," said Orla, sounding more like the adult than the child. This was part of a world that Orla was familiar with.

"Yes, it is," Maeve replied with feeling,

"and I would really like everything to slow down, but somehow I don't feel that I can take the time to process this. It's like stepping on to a moving platform that started to accelerate as soon as I stepped onto it. "

Orla hesitated before saying,

"You are right, something is happening, I have been feeling it too. I called Ada last night, to ask her what I should do. She was her cryptic self, and said you might be the key. Are you?" They looked at each other, both lost in thought but communicating their disquiet.

The waitress interrupted with an, "avec ceci?", which was a 'do you want anything else or are you finished and can I have the table back' question. Tension relieved, Maeve and Orla smiled, paid the bill, and left. It was not long after midday, but equally there was not enough time to make it worthwhile for Orla to 'shlep' back to school, so they chose to use the time for themselves. With no shopping to be done, Orla suggested that she help Maeve figure out what had happened to Kamal.

"Let's physically go up to the Uni and ask them, and see what we can find out? We can tell them you want to inspire me to continue my education. Then we can ask questions without raising any suspicions", she said.

Keen not to dissuade Orla, Maeve added

"Not a bad idea. But really I want to know about Kamal, if he was a student there? And did he finish his course? If he didn't, then do they know what happened to him".

Orla thought for a moment then,

"Why don't we take a two pronged approach? You can say you are doing some research for a book, and I can say I am looking at colleges? We split up and attack from two different perspectives, and then go home and compare notes?"

At least it sounded active, and they both needed to stop thinking and start doing.

As they walked up the long incline from town to the University campus, Maeve had a question for Orla, "this may sound a little strange but, your bed is made every morning..?"

Orla was quick to answer, with clear signs of guilt,

"Yes, Mum, I know, you are amazing, I promise I will start doing it from now on."

That was that then, it had been Edward all along, Maeve smiled ruefully to herself. She wasn't sure what to do about him but given how helpful he was, it clearly wasn't urgent, and she wasn't about to let Orla off the hook just yet either.

Then on a more serious note, she made Orla promise that she would talk to her Dad that evening. He was a hairdresser in Arras, in Nord Pas de Calais, where he had his own business 'Vandam's Salon for Men'. Maeve and Pascal got on fine.Their relationship had faded out while Maeve's father had been ill, and she and the children had moved over to the UK to be with Ada. At some stage, Pascal met an adoring younger woman, who was probably better for him. Now he had his hands full with four children under 10 years old. Orla and Marianne spent most of their time with Maeve, because in Canterbury they had their own rooms, and the house was pretty quiet. They all got on, any blame had dissolved over the years, and like so many, they had adapted to become a new larger family.

They turned off the Whitstable Road, passing the burned out shell of a building at the entrance to the campus, and on into the large green parkland surrounding the university buildings. The University of Kent is a plate glass university founded in the mid 1960s. During construction they unearthed traces of an extensive medieval pottery at Tyler Hill some of which may have gone back to Roman times, there was nothing to suggest that history in the nondescript sprawl of buildings there now.

Arriving a little out of breath, from the walk up the hill, they split up. Orla went to admissions, and Maeve went to the Department of Astronomy, Space Science and Astrophysics, where she found out, they did indeed have a course module on Rocketry and Human Spaceflight.

Orla did pretty well, blagging her way through the admissions process, plus she really did want to know about their policies on recycling, and their approach to supporting students seeking to create a better world. Then she brought in her emphasis on how they handled foreign students. Carla, the admissions officer was getting exasperated, and by now almost at the end of her tether, she was looking round for an escape route when she spotted some colleagues. She called out,

"Tony, have you got a moment? You do some of the extra curricular activities with the students, don't you? We have a young lady here very keen on the University's student policies, and how we engage with the local community. Can you help?"

She finished with a pleading look, indicating that this was a tricky customer who had tested her beyond her regular sales pitch. Tony was amused, and enjoyed a challenge, so answered with

"Sure, we have few minutes. Meet Adam, one of my PhD students. In fact, I am just trying to convince Adam to join in some of the extras available here in Canterbury."

Carla, pleased with herself, made the introduction with an air of 'you should be impressed with the lecturers we have here. Not just clever but handsome too.' She said,

"Meet Dr. Tony Blackstone, senior lecturer in Archeology, who I am sure can answer all of your questions." With that she handed Orla a prospectus, left them at her desk, and disappeared, possibly on her coffee break.

Orla did think Adam was pretty hot, but equally this probably wasn't the right occasion. As a local, Orla didn't want to hear about the benefits of University life in Canterbury, and was pretty confident that this conversation wasn't going to help her find out about Kamal. So, making her best excuses, she cut the chat short and left.

. . .

As with the hospital, no one would give Maeve any specific or detailed information, data protection, GDPR etc. Before she left, Maeve had decided to have a look around, and see if there was anything that might help. She looked at the notice boards and all the posters, mostly cool images of rockets and space flights, or amazing things students had done. It was all pretty recent, so having almost given up, she got a real start when something jumped out at her from a smaller older image. Now she would have something to tell Steve!

CHAPTER 11

THE SECOND TIME

Canterbury is small enough for you to trip over the same people more than once. But when the snatch of conversation is about you twice, it makes you think. Maybe we just like the same rich roast. For whatever reason, it brought me back to the weeks following Susan's death. Her body was relatively light, I moved her over to the edge of the park under the trees. I didn't feel the need to rush. I altered her body so that it would look like it had been dumped. I liked the drama of it. It suggested a crime of passion. I took one of her earrings, which added to the staging. I also wanted a keepsake. I wanted a reminder of that strange feeling that came over me, when I knew that I had killed her.

Back home that night, with a glass of red wine, and good music, I chose the St Matthew Passion. I reflected on what had happened, and what might happen now. I felt calmer and more at peace than ever before. This was good to know. The park had been empty, there were no witnesses. The grass was tall enough that it might be some time before anyone discovered the body, you had to be quite close before you could see anything at all. I had been clever to move it. Would they find me? I wasn't worried, it felt almost as if it was a game happening to someone else. Over the next few weeks I waited. The news coverage, the police investigation all made the adrenaline flow. I wasn't afraid, I was excited. I was waiting for a knock on the door, but it never came. The news reports suggested that it was a 'domestic', that the killer was most likely known to the victim and that possibly an unhappy relationship, a fight that went too far. So my little scene setting had worked. I began to feel elated. Time passed. No one came looking for me. My story had been well prepared but I never got to use it.

Months turned to years I knew that they would never work it out. I think I was a little disappointed.

As the time passed the excitement leached away. Life returned to the ordinary, it became flat. I wanted that feeling of heightened senses of being truly alive. I began to feel the need to kill again, would it give me the same kick as before? I took time to plan a crime that looked like an accident. I enjoyed the planning, if I was careful I would be able to kill whenever I needed to. Pick up someone with no ties, make it look like a road accident which research had shown is the most common cause of unusual deaths. Each detail gave me a thrill. Choose a road with no cameras or witnesses. I found the perfect location just off the motorway.

For months I would go over to Folkestone train station and hang about with the minicab drivers till I was able to mimic them, which wasn't hard. At first that was thrilling enough, knowing that at any time I might find my victim. It also gave me time to perfect my side of the story. I wore black so as not to stand out. I got a flat cap to shade my face from anyone who came too close. I found out where to park so that the station cameras couldn't fully make out the number plate.

Now the need was growing, I could feel the tension rising, I was short with people, small things could set me off making me very angry, less in control. I was beginning to think that I would never spot the perfect target when one Friday night he arrived. Just right. Foreign looking. I knew him but my disguise was good enough to fool him. Enough time in the car to get him to confirm that no one was waiting for him in the UK. In the end the car 'accident' was messy, not as controlled, not as satisfying. Nevertheless afterwards, I experienced that same sense of relief, of calmness. As if it had burst something building inside me and all the tension that had been building up flowed away.

. . .

As a proof of concept it worked well, there was no follow up, no investigation. I destroyed all of his bags, I took them to be incinerated but at the waste care centre they convinced me that it was better to recycle them. More appropriate I thought. Clothes shredded or if dangerous plastic, then bundled up to pollute China, either way all disposed of, no traces.

CHAPTER 12

AND THEN IT ALL STARTED TO ADD UP

Maeve decided that it was time for a full family pow-wow. No more secrets. It was only a fifteen minute walk downhill from the University. On the way she called Ada to see if she could come round for supper,

"Its only pasta and salad, no meat because Orla's gone veggie, but I guess you know that already."

Maeve wanted to reconcile her relationship with Ada but at the same time she was jealous that Orla had gone to her grandmother instead of her. Old habits are hard to change and Maeve realised what she was doing as the words came out of her mouth; she knew she could do better

"Ada, I'm sorry I didn't mean it to come out like that. We would really like you to come over. There are family things that I would like you to be here for. Orla told me that she can see spirits too, so you were right, I don't need to go through this alone and now I hope we can work together, in fact all three of us can work together."

Ada almost hooted with joy,

"Hurray! At last! Maeve, love, you have made me very happy! Listen, I was thinking of dropping into 'Clothesline', and the parking round there is tricky, if I come over now will you come in with me?"

Maeve wasn't sure if this was a peace ploy from Ada or she really wanted a lift. They both loved stylish clothes but designer prices were out of their league so their favourite place was Clothesline in Canterbury.

As soon as she heard the plan Orla was up for it too, she had the same sense of drama as Ada and preloved clothes were definitely the way forward. Bonding over shopping was ideal, Maeve just hadn't thought of vintage or second hand for Orla. Every time Maeve had a new event or film festival to work on she would buy her 'opening night' outfit here so they were regulars, the three of them together would almost fill the shop.

On arrival the always immaculately dressed Pam was dealing with a difficult customer who thought her Phase 8 work jacket was smart enough for the shop and couldn't see why Pam wouldn't sell it for her. Maeve, always ready to stand up for people in trouble, wasn't just going to look the other way. She caught Pam's eye, and stood by the counter ready for moral support or whatever else was needed. Orla and Ada had already gone downstairs and their conversation wafted up,

"Silk kimonos, an essential item in any woman's wardrobe.."

Pam was placating her customer,

"I'm sorry but in spring we look for bright colours, black is more for the autumn/winter collection".

The stand off upstairs ended with a face saving

"We'd be happy to try it after the summer", and as the woman turned to leave, Maeve took in her well dressed appearance and it occurred to her that she had seen her somewhere before. Had she been in the cafe when she was waiting for Steve? It was a fleeting thought, she felt familiar, and not in a pleasant way.

. . .

That evening, the call with Pascal went very well. He had never been in favour of college, the concept of apprenticeships suited him better. His most useful comment was,

"With Orla when she knows what she wants to do she will do it. That girl has the willpower to move mountains, never underestimate her!"

But they all agreed on one thing. Orla should finish her exams this summer, at least then she would have her GCSEs.

Satisfied after good food, they settled down around the table over fresh mint teas and decaf coffees, without the need to say anything specific, they knew that they were a stronger group than they had been for years. Having realised that she had completely missed the significance of Orla's growing concerns, Maeve was now trying to be sensitive to Marianne's reactions to the various happenings and momentous life decisions.

Marianne's first response had been,

"I am so glad I don't have this 'gift'! You can do all that and leave me out of it."

Maeve wondered if that was a bit too glib, maybe masking her disappointment as not being included in this special club. She decided to try to get Marianne on her own rather than confront her with the others there before digging any deeper.

Marianne's insights into her sister were more in tune with her growing maturity,

"Orla should do what she needs to. You know Orla, when or if, she decides she wants to get grades and go to college, she will find a way. But I know what she has been going through recently and it's not for her right now. I am happy for you that it's out in the open, no secrets is a very good principle, and that goes for you too Mum!."

Orla beamed, enjoying her turn at being the centre of attention. Having resolved these issues at least on a temporary basis Maeve turned the conversation,

"Can we share what we have 'heard' over the last few days? Ada and Orla, you both said you were getting messages.

I am still really new at this so, what were they and how did you get them?"

Ada enjoyed regaling them with all of her 'war' stories. For Ada this was the first time that the whole family believed her, and were hanging on every word, with Maeve taking notes. Marianne withdrew and was clearing up and getting ready for school, trying to get things back on track. Maeve didn't notice, she was focused on Ada,

"...and another thing, they are not good at time, I mean spirits often think something has just happened when it was years ago. They seem to get caught in a time loop until you can set them free. This can be very useful, because you don't have to say 'wait a moment I'll get back to you', you don't say anything, you just agree with the spirit and if it takes years for you to do whatever they need that's fine. They go round and round not knowing that any time has past at all. Oh,"

Ada took a deep sigh,

"there are so many things I have to tell you, but there's no rush. We can take it a step at a time."

The next morning Steve was first at the cafe, he had his coffee in front of him and when Maeve tried to order hers, the barista said,

"it's okay, he's already ordered, and paid! I'd hang on to him if I were you, we get some weirdos in here but he is definitely one of our nicest customers. I'll bring it to you in a jiffy".

Steve was feeling chuffed, he had got some information, and wanted some admiration so he could do his 'it was nothing, it's just what we do, all in a day's work', routine. The rug was pulled from under him when Maeve sat down with a

"You won't believe what I found yesterday up on the campus!"

Oh well, his turn would come.

"Go, on, don't stop there".

"Just like with the hospital I couldn't officially get access to any of the records for confirmation, or even any information to give us dates, the only thing they would do is to verify a degree but you have to have the exact name and dates, plus there is a £12 charge. I thought it would be in the public domain if someone qualified from a University, so that the employers could check their CV.... Anyway I am getting distracted, as I was leaving I saw this."

Steve had been patiently waiting for her to get to the point when at last she pulled out her phone and showed him the photo that she had taken, of the picture on the notice board. It was of an old, scruffy, and probably forgotten picture that had been up for some years. The faded colours were moving towards the yellow end of the spectrum, but the faces were clear enough. There they were. Susan *and* Kamal. Part of a group of students who had launched a model rocket into space. They were laughing, happy, it looked like they were having some very student goofy fun. On closer inspection you could just make out, someone older, who looked like a lecturer, in the background.

"When I got home, I looked it up online and it was taken in 2011 just before Susan was murdered. So my detective work says that they knew each other! Is that a strange coincidence or something more sinister?"

Maeve took a sip of her coffee as she waited for his reaction. Steve seemed to like to think before he spoke, pause,

"That's very interesting."

'Understatement of the year', thought Maeve. He went on,

"I found some information too. You left the bag on the table when you dashed off yesterday. By the way, I'd like to hear more about that too. Why the sudden dash, I don't think I said anything and I wouldn't want you to think I was trying to make a move too soon?"

The colour began to rise in Maeve's cheeks, she carefully studied her coffee and began to stir it unnecessarily. She didn't look up but feeling the need to fill the gap in conversation she blurted,

"It was my younger daughter Orla, who should have been at school. She and her older sister are both doing their big exams this year, I worry, and not without reason, but that's another story. Go on, what did you find out?"

"After you departed in haste and you left the bag with me. I went through it and the date of Kamal's visa is from September 2014. There was also a ticket stub in the wallet so he got the train on 19th Sept which was a Friday. I checked and the University term started on 29th September, he probably planned on having the week to settle in before starting his studies. Then I cross-checked with our records and that 'hit and run' I told you about. It was on the 19th Sept. Actually the body was discovered on the Saturday, the 20th Sept, but the autopsy placed the accident the night before."

Silence, they looked at each other, allowing the implications to sink in.

Maeve started,

"So are we thinking that the facts and the visit from my friend in the spirit world are beginning to stack up?"

Steve was unwilling to agree, but in spite of himself he nodded his affirmation. Maeve continued,

"We have also ascertained that victim number one knew victim number two even if the deaths were separated by a little over three years?"

Steve nodded again.

"I don't know how you do things in 'police world', but it seems to me like the worst case scenario here is that we are looking at a serial killer in this very area who may still be active!"

CHAPTER 13

SHOCK OF A DIFFERENT KIND

Now Maeve was really in her element. They ordered more coffee, the waitress gave Maeve a wink, as she carefully placed her flat white on the table. Maeve hoped Steve hadn't noticed. There were lists to be written. Work to be divided between them. What information would need the police to access and what information could Maeve get herself. Would they need a warrant? Did she need to talk to her spirit contacts, the victims, and if so how would she do that? She'd need to check in with Ada for that.

Maeve had not stopped talking when she noticed something flash across the screen of her mobile phone, there was a missed call, actually there were 14 missed calls on her mobile phone.

"Give me a minute." She said as she called voicemail. Suddenly she went rigid, turned white and almost dropped the phone. Not able to talk, tears streamed down her face. Steve had been a copper long enough to know the kind of information that caused this level of reaction, and it wasn't good.

He moved to her side of the table and put his arm around her shoulders, she needed a shoulder to cry on. Giving her a few minutes, very gently and calmly he said,

"Was it the hospital?"

She nodded.

"Was it Canterbury hospital?"

She shook her head, and mumbled

"William Harvey, Ashford."

Steve was really good in a crisis, he constructed a scenario from the info he had, it was likely that something bad had happened to Maeve's mother, if it had been the daughters it would be more likely to be the local hospital. Maeve was clearly in a state of shock. Steve took charge of the situation,

"You're not in a fit state to drive, I'll take you there now."

She nodded again, still deathly white. Half supporting her they left the cafe. Steve hadn't mentioned that they would be on a motorbike, Maeve didn't even seem to notice, she was lost on some level of autopilot. Steve was hugely sympathetic. He had had enough of this kind of bad news himself but at the same time having an attractive woman need him, felt good, and he always enjoyed the bike ride through the green countryside.

He felt her body warm behind him on the bike, and in his head he could hear The Eagles, playing 'Take it Easy'. They passed the fields of apple trees in blossom, the hops beginning to climb up the vertical strings, the river still full but not overflowing, the bizarre pointed oast houses and sleepy farmhouses, all idyllic almost in spite of the purpose of their drive. Apart from the roar of the bike which meant no conversation, it was a peaceful twenty-five minutes giving them both time to reflect.

The message from the hospital was

"Maeve McPhillips, I am very sorry to tell you that your mother Ada McPhillips has had a serious heart attack and is in intensive care about to undergo emergency surgery. We have tried to get in touch with you, but since there was no reply we have gone ahead. She has already been anaesthetised. You do not need to rush over here, it will be at least four hours before we know if the surgery has been successful. We suggest that you take that time and make your way calmly to the hospital, the William Harvey, accident and emergency unit. Reception will be able to direct you from there."

Maeve couldn't process it. She couldn't lose Ada now, not now, when after all these years they had begun to find each other. All that wasted time. Maeve wasn't religious but on that journey she held onto Steve like a protective barrier, and prayed to any god that would listen. 'Please, please, God, let her come through. I need her!' She surprised herself with the level of emotion. Ada had always been there, sometimes like a needy 'prima donna', but always there. They had had their differences, Maeve had spent years blaming Ada for everything wrong in her life. Now faced with the possibility of losing her, Maeve was enveloped in an overwhelming, indescribable, sadness, she didn't 'need' her, she loved her. She loved Ada's quirky ways; the flamboyant outfits, the drama and colour that surrounded her. In her mind Maeve ran through so many of the good times they had had. Ada making her laugh, Ada turning ordinary life into fun adventures. She didn't want to break down in tears again so Maeve concentrated all her thoughts, 'Please, whatever spirit or god is out there, please, please, don't let her die.'

They hadn't been able to speak on the way. When Steve parked the bike he took her straight to accident and emergency reception. It was only then that he found out his assumptions had been right. By the time they got there, Ada had gone into surgery.

The hospital had carried out an angiogram and discovered that Ada had serious plaque, or fat, build-up around her heart with arterial blockages of more than 70% in three of her arteries. Probably not helped by 35 years as a heavy smoker along with a fondness for a few glasses of red wine in the evening, every evening. Multi-vessel coronary artery disease is high risk, the prognosis was that she needed three of her four coronary arteries dealt with immediately. The surgeon was going to insert stents to open up the valves and allow normal blood flow. The planned insertion of a stent has become a reasonably low risk operation needing only a day in hospital for the whole process. For Ada, with three stents and under emergency conditions the risk was high. Nothing for it but to wait.

Steve got her that emergency standby of hot tea with plenty of sugar, explaining that adrenaline uses up a lot of energy and that soon she would also need to eat something or she would suffer a sugar crash and get the shakes, but right now the sugar was fine as a temporary stop gap. Maeve let it all drift over her, the ordinariness of the words with his reassuring voice was just what she needed, and he knew that. The tea was good too.

Then she began to talk. Steve was a good listener. Maeve drifted from subject to subject. How she had grown up in Southern Ireland, in Co. Meath, race horse country,

"It's green, really green, everything is green, lush vegetation that merges into the trees so there is no gap in the greenness. You don't realise it till you leave and then when you come back you can see it, there really are forty shades of green. And why is it so green, I hear you ask, because it rains, a lot! But when the sun comes out it is a beautiful, rich colour, you can smell the earth, the wild flowers, delicate white of the cow parsley in the hedgerow"

She was talking, just to talk. She rambled on, the family had moved to England when Maeve's father got a job in Middlesex. They lived in London because Ada had had enough of the countryside for a while. Maeve didn't talk much about her father, clearly they had had a strained relationship. Moving on to her life now,

"I don't know. Since I had the girls I think I put my own life on hold. I seem to have been surviving, just managing from day to day, focusing on making sure they had a good childhood, being there for them. When my Dad was ill, dying, I didn't deal with it, I thought about supporting Ada, supporting the kids. I didn't want to think about 'me'. This year was a big year for me, the big 'four oh', so I have been doing a serious stock take, I have begun to realise that rather than face up to things I have been putting them off. These last few days have forced me to face up to so many aspects of my life.

"I didn't know, or I had refused to acknowledge, that I could communicate with the other side. My daughters are growing up and I am not sure what's going on anymore."

Maeve was talking herself out, but for the first time in a long time it felt comfortable, no one was judging her, Steve really was a good listener. She appreciated it. More tea.

Slowly Maeve was beginning to register her surroundings; the hot dry air that is the same in all hospitals, the sweet smell of disinfectant, clean, dry, white and pink, safe. She noticed that there were a few people behind Steve. They looked like they were waiting to talk to her.

She was just about to say something when a woman called out,

"Ms McPhillips, Ms McPhillips?" Locating Maeve, she went on,

"I'm Dr Dalrymple, your mother's cardiologist. Is this your husband?" Addressed to Steve,

"emm, no a friend…" No need for explanations,

"Fine, first of all, good news, well so far so good. She has come through the operation and is in the recovery unit. So long as there is no infection it should be fine. She seems a little disoriented, talking to people who aren't there. It does happen, we expect it will pass in the next day or so. Will you be able to look after her?" Not waiting for an answer she ran on,

"We will keep her in for observation for the next 24 hours. All being well, you can then take her home, as soon as she is fully discharged. She should not be on her own for the next few weeks. She will feel like she has a lot more energy, so be careful and don't let her do too much, but recovery can be surprisingly quick."

Inside Maeve had been doing a little dance, on the outside she had clenched her fist so hard that her nails dug into the palms of her hands and she had changed colour a few times, now her cheeks now in full bloom.

"Thank God! Fantastic, fantastic!! When can I see her?"

Dr Dalrymple had a broad smile, it's good to be able to give good news,

"Don't get too excited yet, we still have to make sure that everything is okay, that the stents have taken and there are no adverse reactions. Sometimes in rare cases the body can reject the material that the stents are made of. Your mother seems to be very resilient, so we are hopeful. You should be able to visit her in an hour or so. I will send someone down to get you as soon as she's ready. But as I said we will keep her in for observation overnight. Oh and by the way..."

The doctor pulled Maeve aside and went on,

"with regards to her other problems, I think we can help, once she has got over this operation, get her to come back and ask for me in person."

Now Maeve was worried,

"What other problems?"

Maeve knew that Ada wasn't the fastest walker in the world and often mentioned her hip.

"Do you mean her hip?"

"Well, if that's what she calls it then yes her 'hip', I can think of much worse terms to describe it! But get her to come back to me. I'm sure she doesn't want to discuss this with more people than she has to"

Wondering what it was that Ada hadn't told her, and making the mental note to have a private talk with Ada, but still beaming Maeve said,

"Thank you Doctor, thank you so much. Amazing, that you have done all that and we didn't even know she was ill!"

The young doctor enjoying Maeve's relief continued,

"She probably didn't know herself. She may have felt less energy and just put it down to age, a lot of people do that, and don't want to bother anyone. You should never do that, always get things checked out. It's much easier for us when it isn't an emergency!"

Dr Dalrymple may have looked young but she had an air

of confidence in her subject that was very reassuring. With that she left them for her next case.

In a quandary over what to do about the girls Maeve sent each of them a text, 'Ada is okay but in hospital for the moment so I may be late back'. She didn't want to frighten them but she did want to prepare them, fingers crossed she had hit the right tone and that would do it.

"Steve, this may sound strange, but is there someone behind you, sort of waiting to talk to me?"

Steve turned around, and then did another turn,

"No, not really, unless you mean that bloke over there." He pointed to a man standing by the hospital shop browsing the flowers.

"Thanks, I think there may be a few new 'friends' here. Can you give me a minute? They won't talk while you are with me."

Now Steve was totally disconcerted, then again, he could do with some air and checking in with the station. He walked out of the hospital, phone in hand, while Maeve sat down at a quiet table notebook in hand,

"It's okay you can talk now."

CHAPTER 14

AND AGAIN

From then on I began to look out for people that the world would be better off without. I realised that as stress built up in my life I would need to kill someone to release it so I spent a lot of my time idly selecting victims. I had wondered if strength was important but in fact skill is the key.

The homeless are pretty easy, few questions asked and often no one even notices that they are missing until some dog walker finds a strange bone or two. I don't even count them, there's no challenge.

Sometimes I would consider work colleagues that I felt hadn't got their job on merit, really quite disposable. They would be likely to leave more clues that would have to be tidied up, not impossible, quite a good challenge. And challenges seemed to increase the excitement and the ultimate release.

Regardless of whom I chose, or choose in the future, I am never going to be a prime suspect, too well spoken. It's one of those things, in England, people still know their place. I mean they talk about equality but when it comes down to it, a posh accent with some jovial banter, will trump the truth any day.

CHAPTER 15

MORE OF THEM...

Steve came back to see how Maeve was doing, he could see that the notebook in front of her had pages of notes and she was still writing. As he got closer, she stopped and looked up,

"Thank goodness you are here, I don't know how to make it stop. But as soon as you appeared they began to step back."

Steve had gone along with the 'talking to spirits' as long as it provided useful information, but he still wasn't completely convinced. This was something different, this time he was experiencing it in real time, or rather he wasn't but he was seeing Maeve go through it. No crystal balls, just a very normal hospital waiting area. What was actually happening? Using his 'interrogation' skills he kept his face and voice in neutral, masking the impatience he felt.

"Would you like to tell me what exactly is taking place?".

When Maeve looked directly at him he could see panic in her eyes,

"It turns out hospitals have a lot of ghosts. I have spoken to three or four of them, most are normal people but some of them are not all that nice, in fact some of them are very unpleasant, and pretty scary, even threatening."

It was clear that someone, or something had frightened her. After a beat, Maeve went on,

"The majority of these spirits are people who never got to say 'goodbye' to their loved ones. They want me to do stuff for them, to bring them closure so that they can rest. The requests are really specific, who I have to give the message to and what they want me to say. You can see, I have names and addresses, it's a bit like a shopping list, and it's getting long!"

Maeve paused,

"there is so much sadness. It's exhausting, draining and it's all a bit much for me especially right now. But I feel guilty, I don't want to let them down and if I can help them find peace, I should do it, shouldn't I?"

Steve could see that she was looking for him to give her a way out, but what could he say? In fact, her distress was the most compelling thing he had seen to make him believe that she was talking to the dead. The very fact that she didn't want this and she wasn't trying to sell hope to people in distress made him think it must be true. However they could discuss beliefs at their leisure, right now they needed to deal with Ada, then get Maeve out of here, get her home, and help her keep it together for the moment. With a quick,

"Lets deal with that later", Steve looked around to see if it was time for Maeve to go to Ada.

Maeve was hesitating over something, she seemed not sure how to put it in words….

"One of the people, spirits, a guy called Kevin was not like the others. I don't know how to explain. He was rude and pushy and very opinionated. Physically he had that almost translucent skin but at the same time looked like he hadn't washed in a long time. You know, someone who doesn't see daylight often. He seemed to know about both Susan and Kamal, not in a good way, more like he knew the 'victims', and what had happened to them, he hinted that he knew the killer! He shouted random comments. 'Sheep-els','I'm not alone', 'the earth will be cleansed' and 'he knew how to fix things', then it felt like he was trying to edge me away from the others, he wanted to get me on my own. And, even more creepy, he said, 'now that we knew each other, he had more stories to tell and would find me again'!"

Before Steve could say anything the nurse who had been looking for Maeve interrupted with,

"Can you follow me? Ada's ready to see you now."

Steve signalled to Maeve that he would wait there and take her back to Canterbury when she was ready.

This was the positive boost Maeve needed, she almost ran after the nurse. Everything else was forgotten, she was on her way to see Ada. Ada would know how to deal with these 'people', Maeve was confident that she could park them for the moment. The feeling of relief flooded her body. Her emotions were in total roller coaster mode. Full of energy now, she wanted to laugh at everything, even if it wasn't funny.

Ada was in the recovery room, lying flat on her back, the nurse was there to monitor her vital signs. As soon as she saw Maeve, Ada tried to get up.

"No Mrs McPhillips! Lie flat until we have your blood pressure under control. You must be the daughter, please don't let her get excited. We want her calm for the moment. She is very lucky to be here and we want to make sure that she recovers. We don't want any relapses here!", the nurse went on over Ada's head in the way you might talk over a naughty child with the explicit intention that the child hears you.

"Maeve, love, it's great to see you, aren't you wonderful to come over straight away! Aren't they marvellous? They got me here and sorted me out just like that. And Nurse Nancy, well I call her Nurse Nancy, some might call her Nurse Ratched, doesn't she have wonderful natural blond curls, shame they have to be tied back. You'd look better darling if you let them loose and keep your hair down, none of that severe tie-back look."

This last bit was addressed to the nurse's back as she was retreating, given the positive readouts on the monitors. Ada turned her head to face Maeve,

"So, what's the story, how long am I in for? When can I go home? I feel great, a bit sore where they put that thing in, but loads more energy. Dying to get up and out."

Grinning from ear to ear Maeve, was enjoying all of this. Ada was fine, sounding like her normal self. Maeve put one hand on Ada's arm avoiding the drip and used the other to take her hand.

"Ada, Mother, Mum, I am so glad you are here. I know you are going to squirm but I have to say this. On the journey over here there were many things I regretted and not saying this was the biggest one. I love you, I have always loved you, now it's time to say it! And I made a decision, right now, today, we will start again, with a real mother daughter relationship."

Ada had rolled her head away and when she turned back Maeve could see her tears.

Ada, "What did you do that for? Ach! I don't even have a tissue and Nurse Ratched will murder me if I get up!"

They both laughed, Ada was forced to remember the operation stopping with an 'ouch' and "oooh, don't make me laugh that hurts!," as Maeve stretched over to the bedside table, pulled out a tissue and wiped Ada's tears.

Taking charge Maeve went on,

"You are in overnight. If the results are good they will discharge you tomorrow. I will come and pick you up when you are ready, but no going to your home. You will have to come to Canterbury for a few weeks convalescence. If you want to recover quickly you will have to do what you are told for a change. Starting with no red wine! That was a major operation, really serious, you nearly died. Well, now things are going to change. Then the doctor mentioned something else and said 'she can help you', which I thought was a bit cryptic. Is there something you haven't told me? Anyway, let's wait till you're home and better, we can fix the world then. "

Maeve thought she might enjoy this. She was right things were going to change, but not necessarily in the way she expected.

CHAPTER 16
WHAT NEXT?

Safely back home, Maeve thought about Steve. She was so grateful to him, but at the same time she didn't know what to say or what to do about him. She wasn't sure what she wanted, what kind of relationship she wanted. Steve had been perfect in a crisis, but Maeve had been going through such a whirlwind of emotions she wasn't sure if her feelings for him were real or hormonal. Can you put something that hasn't really happened on hold? Would he understand? As she had done so many times before when she wasn't ready to face her emotions, she turned to the practical.

There were urgent things to sort out, to be able to bring Ada home. A camp bed in the sitting room, bed linen and towels, bedside table and light, nightlight, TV moved into the breakfast/dining room which was a precaution to avoid any potential complaints. Edward had appeared in the middle of the preparations fussing around, he didn't like change, and would move things back to where they were. Maeve had to take a minute out to go through it with him and explain how, now she could see him, how much she appreciated him. She did wonder if he could become a problem.

"Well, you are kind m'lady, and when there are kind people in the house I like to help make a happy atmosphere. When they are not kind I can do things to make life difficult.

Knives work. Also spontaneous combustion, or fire. I have heard them say 'poltergeist' but it isn't true, it's just me."

Edward added, if it hadn't come with such a broad smile, and an 'at your service' bow, might have been a threat. Now Maeve knew that she was the only one who could see him, she had decided that she wasn't going to introduce him to the others yet until she was completely sure he was all good.

Then there was the online research into Ada's condition and best after care, Marianne and Orla took that on. They had even colour coded menus and exercise sheets for Ada, which Ada would, of course, hate.

The relief that Ada had come through, gave them the positive energy they needed to bring them together. The preparations were mixed with the recounting of Ada adventures, 'do you remember when' stories.

Maeve had started with,

"When I was nine, she gave me a multicoloured feather duster as my birthday present. Even funnier was that I loved it!"

Marianne added, "That time she mistook the raw liver pate for chocolate mousse and took a sneaky spoonful",

and Orla joined in with

"how many times have you opened a box of chocolates to see some with bites taken out of them where Ada had been 'just testing'."

All of them were laughing at the memories, but Maeve had worked herself into a state where she was shaking so much with mirth she couldn't get another story out. Clearly the relief and the pleasure in doing things together were more the cause of the giddiness than anything actually that funny. In the end a Chinese takeaway was ordered-in and of course they overindulged, all three ended the day exhausted, overfed, but happy. Reports from the hospital were good, she was still due to be discharged around midday the next day.

The next morning the first thought in Maeve's mind after checking in on Ada, was trying to work out what to do about Steve. Probably better to try to cool things for the moment, she needed to get her emotions more under control. When in doubt 'wait and see' was always a good policy.

Sometimes personal crises bring people together, sometimes the gratitude causes awkwardness, and sometimes the crisis acts as a reminder of a bad time best forgotten. Steve wasn't sure which camp he fell into. He also didn't know what he wanted. Having a relationship was great in the abstract, but after so many years he had got used to his own company and wasn't sure that he was ready to have someone around all the time. He needed his own space. He needed time to think but he didn't get it.

By the time he had arrived at the station word had gone round that he had a new woman, bint, bird, or bit on the side. Steve was known for not rising to the bait, teasing him was a normal part of station life and this was too good to miss. True to his reputation, he ignored it all, getting back to unfinished paperwork. It didn't mean that he didn't care, in fact it bothered him how much it annoyed him and how much he wanted to deny it. He had given Maeve his personal mobile number, but she hadn't called. It seemed ridiculous to him but having decided that really he needed his own space he now began to feel like a teenager again, should he call her? Was she waiting for him? Thinking it through, Maeve would have a lot to deal with today, best leave it for the moment, and laugh off the ribbing. Putting his phone down on his desk, he saw the message.

Maeve started the day with a spring in her step. The house was ready, she would do the grocery shopping on her way over to the hospital in Ashford. 'What to feed Ada? Start with comfort food, baked potatoes and homemade coleslaw, no grated cheese or minimal butter, should be okay and easy to prepare. Or something an invalid could eat, homemade brown bread with a boiled egg? That would do it.' It was

Maeve's own favourite food when she needed to recover from anything. Decision made, she had the morning to herself. Time to go for a walk in the University grounds, lovely open space, and unlikely to meet anyone, time for a morning coffee up at the Gulbenkian cafe, plus pick up a spinach and feta pastry takeaway for lunch, she would get one for Ada just in case the hospital food wasn't up to much.

She would send Steve a message, as soon as she had worked out what to say. Walking is a good way to think through things. She decided not to deal with all the 'other world' requests from the hospital spirits until she had spoken to Ada. I mean, do you just phone people up and say I have a message for you from your dead aunt or dead brother? Seemed a bit brutal and they probably wouldn't believe her. There must be a protocol to follow.

Steve held up the piece of paper and shouted out,

"Am I the only one allocated to dealing with this?"

No reply.

"Christ!"

It was a report on a missing person dated yesterday, it had been phoned in while Steve was out. It wasn't really his area, he was a detective but also a nice guy so often offered to help colleagues. Because he loved his motorbike and everyone knew that, they sometimes asked him to do things that were easier on a bike than in a car. This was clearly one of those. It should have been a simple ask. He had to contact the family, ideally he would shoot out to see them asap. He needed to do a risk assessment, meaning, work out how likely they were to come to harm. He liked to do it in person and see the environment that the missing person had left. It should have been done as soon as the report came in. He should have been there to do it. It probably wasn't urgent, but he liked to keep on top of things when he could. It was a young woman, called in by the family. These often sorted themselves out. It was coming close to exam time and sometimes the stress made kids do crazy things, sometimes they run away from one parent to go to the other. Anyway, now, it needed to be sorted right away.

As Maeve left the house, she turned to go up to the University, when suddenly Susan came into her mind and she felt bad, she hadn't tried to contact her and it was all due to Susan that Maeve had met Steve. Maybe a quick walk to Beverly Meadow would be just as good. She had been drinking too much coffee anyway. As she walked purposefully down the hill she wondered how do you get in touch with a spirit? Apart from a seance or one of Ada's gatherings she really didn't know. When she got to the park she thought 'this is easier than I imagined'. Susan was standing there waiting for her. On reaching her Maeve started with, "can we sit down on the bench, I have a lot to tell you? I wasn't sure you would be here."

Susan nodded and said,

"Well perhaps you shouldn't be surprised, I called you, that's why you came."

Actually Maeve was very disconcerted at the idea that the spirit had called her. Trying to dismiss it, Maeve filled Susan in on her meetings with Steve. She skipped out the episode with Ada. Susan had been nodding slightly throughout as though she knew all of it already and was politely waiting for Maeve to finish. But Maeve still had questions,

"Who are you? I mean what were you doing in Canterbury? What about your family? You didn't ask me to do any of the normal family things the others asked, why?"

Susan smiled, "I was told you were a 'friend' and when I first saw you I knew that to be true. You are. But we don't have time for this at the moment, one day I will, but right now you must talk to Steve."

This time Maeve was ready, notebook in hand, Susan went on,

"Steve is looking for someone, tell him that it is serious

and that he must look harder, not too far from here" and she waved her arm in a general direction away from the city centre and that broadly covered Maeve's house, the University and a good twenty percent of the North of Canterbury.

"What has happened? Where exactly?" Maeve was getting better at thinking of the specific info that she would need when reporting back.

Susan looked vague

"I don't know, I am feeling negative energy, distress, and I know it is connected to me. It's that way, over there somewhere." She followed with the same pretty unspecific wave.

"Right now that's all I know. There is a person who needs Stephen. I hope he gets there in time."

Without hesitation, Maeve picked up her phone and rang Steve. When he answered he was sharp and to the point,

"I can't talk, I am on my way to a job, it's near you. I'll call as soon as I arrive, in about ten minutes."

He rang off. Maeve was about to relay this to Susan when she realised that she was on her own again. Feeling helpless she thought 'what now? Nothing I can do till he calls', so she headed home.

Steve had been doubly concerned when he read the address. He had actually been right there yesterday. It turned out Steve's job was at the house next door to Maeve's.

As Maeve walked towards her house she saw Steve getting off his police motorbike parked outside of Anne and Ray's house. What was going on? She caught his attention just as he rang the doorbell.

"Coffee when you're done?".

Steve nodded 'yes' as Ray opened the door. Maeve, not wanting to be nosey slipped out of sight behind the giant rhododendron that separated the two houses.

Maeve got on really well with her neighbours. Lots of

garden chat over the fence. They both liked growing their own veg, often swapping whatever was in abundance like cucumber for garlic, or handing on any excess seedlings in spring. These were the best kind of neighbours. A retired couple, Anne and Ray, had put up with Maeve's family over the years with tolerance and good grace. Marianne and Orla had done a lot of growing up there, from rumbustious play as smaller children, to their adolescence scenes now. There were times when without any awareness of other people, the girls could be the source of ear splitting shrieks of laughter that shattered the neighbourhood peace. They had climbed the neighbours trees, threatening to break branches or limbs, and now it was loud music at unsociable hours. They would have annoyed Maeve, if they had been her neighbours, but it was all tolerated without complaint by next door, not a peep.

"Children have to grow up, and it's lovely to see and hear the young ones", was all Anne ever said.

Anne was the one who talked to Maeve, she enjoyed a chat over the garden fence. Ray was quiet, mostly nodding in agreement to whatever Anne said. Once a tennis ball shot straight through a pane of glass in their greenhouse door and the only comment was 'no one was hurt', and when Maeve offered to pay to repair it, Anne said

"It was old and needed new glass anyway, this will make Ray do it at last", as she handed Maeve another cucumber.

By the time Steve rang the bell, Maeve had imagined any number of scenarios, she was sufficiently worried about next door and Susan's warning that she hadn't wound herself up about Steve. Cafetière at the ready, she waved at the mugs, biscuits, milk and sugar with a 'help yourself' gesture as she launched non-stop into

"I have just seen Susan again, in the park, she called me because she has a message for you. I wrote it down. Susan's message is, 'regardless of what you think, this is really serious, you must look harder and whoever they are, they are near here, and it's urgent'."

Maeve ended with a flourish, stabbing her notebook. At

first Steve didn't reply. He fiddled with the coffee as he thought about what he should do, then he said,

"I think you should go next door and talk to your neighbour. At the moment I can not tell you why I am here. He may tell you and then we can talk."

In spite of the intel Maeve already had, whether from Susan or somewhere else, Steve knew he had to do this by the book. If something went wrong Maeve might become implicated. Putting that unpleasant thought aside Steve tried to return to more normal conversation,

"How's Ada? Are you going to pick her up today? If so why not meet me on your way over if 'Ray'" Steve looks down at his notebook for confirmation of the name, "if Ray, tells you what happened."

Maeve working out the timing said,

"Sure let's meet at the Lunch Box on Dover St, I'll text you when I'm en route."

Maeve really didn't want to ask Ray what had happened. Putting two and two together, with a sinking feeling she was coming to the conclusion that Anne was the person that Susan was trying to help.

CHAPTER 17

ANNE IS MISSING

Steve got back to the station and was typing up his notes hoping that Maeve would text him soon. He needed the maximum background info he could gather to assess whether this was a person at 'significant risk' of coming to harm, or a case that came under the 'no apparent risk (absent)' heading and just needed monitoring. If it was the former, and he thought it was, he should report it to the Super immediately.

As a detective he didn't normally deal with 'mis-per's' or as he should say 'missing persons' his colleagues the police inspector should handle them. They didn't get on, so when handing the notes over, Steve wanted to be very clear and get everything right. As he looked back at the note he had received he saw the mistake that the desk duty officer had made. The report said 'young woman' so probably lower risk, whereas in fact it should have read 'Mrs Young, woman…' It was her name, Anne Young, and the husband didn't want anyone to know that she had started showing signs of dementia. That put her into a higher risk category. Ray, the husband, said they were keeping the dementia to themselves for as long as they could, hadn't even told the children so when she didn't come home he thought she might just have taken the wrong turning. Ray had explained

"It's not really noticeable yet, but when she makes a mistake she gets flustered and that can make it a lot worse, so I thought if she made a few wrong turns she would have got herself really lost."

Anne was in her seventies and still very active. She should be fine. The real problem was that Ray had waited almost 24 hours before calling it in. Tonight would be her second night in the open. Whatever Maeve knew, or had heard, it was absolutely right, it was urgent. Luckily the weather had been pretty mild but still the effects of exposure would further disorientate Anne. Plus she was not that warmly dressed, he had a note of a lightweight bright pink fleece, no coat . Ray had been in such a state when he was talking to Steve, that Steve hadn't got much more useful information. Ray kept repeating himself,

"She's a walker, she's fit, she's just on a long walk, she'll come through that door in a minute and ask what's all the fuss about."

But she hadn't. When she was late home, Ray had gone out and walked all her usual routes, then all the other possible roads in about a mile radius. By the time he had talked to Steve, he was utterly worn out.

As Steve typed, he thought, she is high risk. He hadn't wanted to send his report to the Super because he should have picked it up earlier, in fact he shouldn't have been doing it at all, it wouldn't look well. Damn it! All this talk about a new woman too. Nothing for it. Steve had always done the right thing no matter how badly it reflected on him.

By the time Maeve left Ray she was drained. The poor man was completely exhausted. Clearly he had been bottling it up inside, all the worries over managing with Anne's dementia and now this. As soon as Maeve asked the right questions it poured out. Maeve made him multiple cups of tea, trying to feed him at the same time, he mustn't have eaten since Anne went missing which wasn't helping. He needed some food and rest. Meanwhile Maeve was keeping an eye on the clock, she didn't want to be late for Ada. When she couldn't put it off any longer she said,

"I have to dash. Why don't you get some sleep to be ready if Anne comes home? You need to eat something and then have a sleep. That sandwich I made is still on the table. Try and have a bite. Then you will be full of beans. I'll only be gone for a few hours. As soon as I get back and get Ada settled, I'll be over and we can sort out shifts so that there is always someone here in case she comes back under her own steam. We can make a plan together."

It was the best she could do for the moment and Ray seemed relieved that he wasn't on his own, and someone was making decisions for him.

As she got into the car, she called Steve, he didn't pick up in time so it went to voicemail.

"Sorry, I can't stop, I'm late. Susan already said it, and I know Anne, I'm convinced that she's in serious trouble, Steve. We need to do something. Maybe if I go door to door? I will get Ray to agree that we have to tell people, I'll get a photo from him, if you don't have one already, we need help. I'm dashing off to get Ada, I'll be on it as soon as I get back.'

Once Ada had come through the operation, Maeve thought her dramas were over, now here she was in the middle of another one. Focus on one thing at a time, she thought, like that old trick of lining coins up on your arm and tossing them into the air, if you catch them one after the other you can get them all, if you try to catch all the coins in one go, you will drop the lot. One at a time. One at a time, and I will get there. At least, thinking that helped her get through the quick shop and drive over to the hospital.

Steve had already emailed his report to the Super, and he copied his colleague, Inspector Tim Houghton, in on the email, which he knew was going to annoy Tim. With a sigh he thought it would be better if he wasn't at his desk when

Tim read it, plus he had a stack of ongoing cases and he needed to check some of the paper files back at HQ. He set off for Maidstone. His support officers at Canterbury station were up to speed and if, or more like when, this needed to be escalated at least he would be able to work with Maeve to get the neighbours involved. Keeping on the case with Tim as the lead, was another matter. Sometimes the best policy was to do what was needed and say sorry later. Maeve would be offline for the next few hours at a minimum. Given the state he was in when Steve left him, he didn't think Ray would be up to organising any local volunteers on his own anyway. Settling his mind on riding the bike perfectly, brought him a sense of peace, and with Jimmy Hendrix's 'Ezy Rider' the perfect bike rider's music running through his head he was at one with the road.

Maeve walked in to the hospital ward to see Ada looking like a film star,

"Wasn't I lucky? The hairdresser and make-up lady were doing their rounds today and I got a total makeover!"

They had moved her to the general ward and she was in her element entertaining the other patients. She wasn't in a rush to go, and as ever had a string of goodbyes and thank-you's to get through. Maeve felt the irritation rise, then she stopped, took a breath, and thought how glad she was that Ada was there. Breathing out slowly allowing the smile to spread across her face, Maeve went to the reception desk to check that they had all the right paperwork, any prescriptions, and that Ada's next outpatient appointment was in order.

"Come on, prima donna, your other public are waiting!" Ada was delighted with all the attention, with a final cheeky,

"Good-bye Nurse Ratched" they left the hospital. Maeve lowered her voice to say,

"Lucky for you most of the staff are too young to remember Nurse Ratched from 'One Flew Over the Cuckoo's Nest'." Ada just laughed,

"Well right now I feel like I could give Jack Nicholson a run for his money!"

In fact Ada didn't need the make-up, the stents had had an amazing effect, the increased blood flow gave her cheeks the healthy glow that had been missing. Seeing the improvement made Maeve realise that Ada had been looking pale and tired, she should have noticed it before. Feeling selfish she was now determined to do better. Maeve knew she would have to break habits formed in childhood to create this new relationship, and made herself a promise to do it now. They had been given a second chance and had to make the most of it. To change the dynamics they really needed something to do, a project, something they could do together, as equals.

Ada was on a roll,

"Maeve darling, we have to go by the house in Sandgate, I have no clothes, no make-up, nothing. I'm quite happy to have a robe and a rice bowl, so long as the robe is Issey Miyake, however I don't think Marianne and Orla would approve. And I need my electric toothbrush, can't live without that!...."

Ada went on and the list got longer, Maeve realised that she was going to be doing the packing with Ada shouting 'helpful' comments; it wasn't going to be easy to keep her promise.

As quick as they could, but longer than planned, Maeve and Ada set off for Canterbury. Ada had taken her favourite soft cushion with the deep purple velvet and Chinese embroidery cover, as a 'make-do' for the back of the car, so that she could 'rest, following doctor's orders on the journey. Actually even though she was clearly revelling in her new role, she did look tired and Maeve was glad to have some time to mull things over herself. They had just crossed the motorway when Maeve heard Ada snore, smiling she knew that Ada's snoring was best not mentioned.

Concentrating on the by-pass after the motorway, Maeve was a little disconcerted when she felt and then heard Kamal, he was sitting in the front passenger seat. Of course, this was his road, his last journey. Given all her recent experiences, this didn't phase Maeve as much as it should have, in fact it felt like seeing a friend,that she was 'getting to know properly'. She was glad that he was there. He started

"It's okay, I know what you have done. You have begun.. that's good. And when it's over and you have found the killer, please tell my story, I am no terrorist, I am just ordinary guy, you saw the photo, we started the rocket society, the 'Space Society'. But maybe you don't know, there are people there at the University who think the earth is flat and that our work is wrong, against their religion, they want to stop us. Not only terrorists are bad people, these conspiracy people are bad people too. But now there is something else I know, and there is more for you to do, and I can help."

CHAPTER 10

QUEEN ADA OR QUEEN MAEVE?

The girls were already back from school by the time Maeve and Ada arrived. The fact that there was no grumbling when asked to help, not even the hint of a 'do I have to?', showed how much they both cared for Ada. In fact they were wonderful, and took over the unpacking and fussing around Ada. So much so that Maeve actually felt comfortable leaving them to it, as she went to drop in on Ray. On her way out she saw Orla trying on Ada's floral orange and pink silk kimono. She just made out Ada saying

"That's not how you tie it darling, here let me show you how you can be spiritual but still sexy, that's better. Gorgeous. You have the best look. Youth!", which was the last word she heard as the door closed.

When Maeve got back home she was on a mission, she filled the others in on the current situation. It was just coming up to 48 hours since Anne had gone missing. Ray had given her permission to share the information and start organising volunteers for a local search. Maeve gave them the low-down,

"Anne is in the early stages of dementia, it was diagnosed a few years ago and they have been fending it off, or at least slowing it down with diet. A daily glass of wine and green vegetables seems to be the core of it.

"Anyway, right now she is at the stage when normally she is okay, just forgetful, but stress causes confusion. So she may be quite close by, but not able to recognise the streets, it's possible that she won't recognise us either.

"I got a reasonable photo of her from Ray. Orla can you scan it? Marianne, while Orla's doing that can you write some text with a contact number and then we should print out, let's say 100 copies? What do you think? And contact number, maybe my mobile?"

Maeve had come to the conclusion that Ray was too distressed at the moment to deal with it other than to physically go and look for her. After he called the police he seemed to think he had done everything. Feeling pretty pleased with how they were getting organised and working as a team, Maeve looked at Ada, who at that moment was actually twiddling her thumbs. She was recovering amazingly well from the operation and clearly wanted to help. Maeve was wondering how to get her involved, make her feel a key player, but not do anything too strenuous.

"Actually, most importantly, Ada, can you go over and look after Ray? He's going to need help telling his kids. They are grown up and living abroad. Once the flyers are printed the rest of us can get a search party going."

It was true, Ada was probably the best person to support Ray. Ada had had a rest, so was happy to freshen up, and go round to Ray,

"Such a nice man. He will need comfort, someone to listen to him. You are right it is crucial that he is not alone at a time like this."

Maeve smiled to herself, giving Ada a critical role was important, and one that in her state she could actually do, was even more important. Maeve felt that she was making progress in considering Ada's feelings.

The girls were on it, fast and efficient. Orla, talking almost to herself as she was working,

"Are you sure we need that many? Don't want any extra waste, but then, this actually is a real case of life or death, so scrub that, 100 copies it is."

Marianne with less talking and more action, was already on her computer sorting out the scan and setting up the layout.

Then Maeve checked in with Steve.

On average Steve had up to twenty cases on the go, that's twenty victims and at least twenty suspects, it meant organising the day in priorities. Urgent versus important. They were all important, and to each of the victims they might be the most important thing in their life, but many of the cases dealt with crimes from some time ago. Urgent meant just that, a crime that was being committed now, or trying to stop a crime being committed.

Steve's career in the police force had taken a few turns over the years. Nearly four years back he had been promoted to Detective Inspector. The promotion was dependent on a move from the Road Policing Unit to CID, Criminal Investigation Department. He spent some time debating whether or not he even wanted the promotion. In CID he was more autonomous, and he got to use his brains, but considerable less time on the bike. But a promotion feels like progress. Once he moved he found the job was stressful, but in the beginning, that had been an exciting challenge. You put the hours in and do the job with care, and you can make a difference.

However over the last few years their numbers had been cut again, so more cases, more stress, but still for the same reward. Lately Steve had even been looking at going private, rather the private companies had been trying to tempt him away from the force. This problem wasn't specific to Steve. In general the police were having difficulty in keeping detectives for the same reasons that Steve was having second thoughts. Too much work, which meant you were not able to do the job you signed up for. The pay wasn't great either, but that wasn't the main reason, it was not being able to do the job, that was depressing.

When Maeve called she went through her plan. Flyers to the neighbours and get them to volunteer, her mobile as the point of contact, as they did the rounds they would attach flyers to any lamp posts or shop windows they could. It was already evening so although they were planning the local walk around now, they didn't think they could do the open spaces or nearby fields till daylight. Ada was acting as Ray's 'representative', meaning she was based next door and could answer any queries or deal with any drop-ins.

"I think we need to be completely in lock-step on this, so can you prepare, but hold off action at your end till we have coordinated our actions here? Give us 20mins and then touch base." He'd told her.

Steve had escalated the case back at HQ. Tim was in control, Steve knew that getting the neighbours to look would be helpful, but he didn't want to hand Maeve over to Tim. This was partly self interest, he didn't want Tim pouring poison into Maeve's ears until he had figured out what relationship they might have. It was now just passed the 48 hour mark so if there was no immediate news they would launch a full scale search. Steve was in the station offering support, working out the planned routes to search, and what they could get *his* volunteers to do.

The spring was becoming early summer and the evenings were lengthening. As there was still some daylight, Maeve said to the girls that she needed a quick walk to stretch her legs while they were doing the flyers. She hadn't wanted to tell them about Kamal's recent visit, she still wasn't that comfortable with the concept.

Kamal had told her she needed to go to their rocket launch site at the University near the dome. Maeve had had to do some quick Googling to find out where that launch site, in the old photo, actually was. It turned out that what had been Parkwood, a green field area, was now luxurious student accommodation. So where, exactly, should she be looking? She headed over to the general area and was lost in thought, when she felt someone close behind her almost touching her shoulder. She jumped.

It was Kevin, the unpleasant guy from the hospital.

"Glad you came to see me. Most of the time I'm in the dark, in the basement, don't see many people down there. Good to come up for a fag break."

Maeve knew that he wasn't there in person but his presence was so strong, she could almost smell his body odour and the stale nicotine clinging to his clothes. He took a drag on the cigarette in his mouth, and bizarrely, Maeve could now smell the fresh smoke. He hadn't stopped talking,

"..so before I tell you anything let's get a few things straight. I am not your friend. I don't give a shit about you, or anyone else. But I know what's what. These smart arses in charge, think they know everything, and I know nothing. Ponces. All fine and dandy, till something doesn't work, the heating, the projector, the internet whatever, then it's all 'Ooooh, Get Kevin, he'll know how to fix it'. Well I do. And I know how to fix a lot more besides."

Maeve really wanted to get away from him, but was concerned that he might follow her. Then she thought, was he the reason Kamal wanted her to come up here? She couldn't see any logical connection and didn't think he was the right source for anything useful. If not, she really didn't have time for this. But then again, maybe he was the one who had crucial information….?

Kev resumed,

"Where were we? Oh yes, those sods who know nothing, but think they're better than me. In the maintenance room I have time and access to the internet. The Uni is part of 'super Janet' our superfast broadband. You can watch anything, find out about anything, there is no censorship, or limits, to what we do on the internet. We had a senior staffer addicted to porn, they didn't do anything, just left him to it!"

He seemed to be rambling, wanting Maeve to listen, so far he hadn't said anything important then,

"I joined some online groups, got some education in what's going on in the 'real world', and found like minded people. That's where I met the killer!"

Maeve's head swung round, he had her full attention now.

"Got you there didn't I?", said with a smug attempt at a laugh, which came out as a cross between a snort and a snigger, before continuing,

"Well, listen up, it's not over yet! I know a lot about it, but if you want to know more, you have to show me some respect, you have to listen to my story. And you have to help me."

Maeve was backing away from him as he spoke, he didn't stop talking

"...Ooh, don't go there, you're going to spoil it all now."

His attitude changed, "No matter, you still need me to solve the mystery. I know a lot about things around here, strange things. But only when you're ready to listen,...."

He wasn't following her, but by the time she realised it she had almost backed into the trees edging the campus. She turned to see where she was going. That's when she saw the body.

CHAPTER 19

THE PINK FLEECE

The pink fleece only just visible, Maeve took in the stillness of the body, but it was the unnatural twist of the head which convinced her that Anne was dead.

Standing stock still, frozen in shock, she thought, what now? On autopilot Maeve fished her phone out of her pocket and called Steve.

"Stay put, don't move, and don't touch anything!"

Steve, already on his way out of the station in Canterbury, roared up to the site on his motorbike, and was there in minutes. He called the info into his team, and backup was on the way, Maeve had said she didn't think Anne was alive, he had called the ambulance they would be needed either way, for resuscitation, or to take the body to the morgue.

She hadn't moved by the time Steve got there. In that moment, he was both a professional police investigator, and concerned 'friend', without hesitation, he gave her a bear hug. The warmth and the energy of the hug, seemed to wake Maeve up. She looked up at Steve, with tears streaming down her face and said,

"We only seem to meet in a crisis."

Steve put his arm around her shoulders,

"It is getting to be a habit, us meeting in emotional circumstances" and smiled.

For a beat they both avoided addressing the situation in front of them. After a pause Maeve added,

"Poor Anne, she didn't deserve this."

First impressions were that Anne had been murdered. There might be circumstantial evidence that they weren't aware of yet, but Steve agreed with Maeve, the angle of the neck was unnatural. There was no sign of anything external that might have caused it.

Steve had time to scan the scene, before the first officer from the station arrived. There was nothing out of place. No footprints that he could see. The grass grows fast at this time of year, so it had probably sprung back into place minutes after the killer had left the scene. The very lushness of the spring this year had hidden the body from any casual passer-by. If they were students or lecturers on their way to class they wouldn't have noticed a thing.

Once the local team arrived, Steve introduced Maeve to Natalie, the police family liaison officer. It seemed like days, but it was only a few hours ago, that Steve had discussed the 'missing persons' case with his Super and Tim. Tim wanted to move Steve to the sidelines, nothing had been formally agreed, yet, but they had both thought it a good idea to bring Natalie on board. Steve needed someone to make sure everything was run by the book, and any personal involvement, wasn't allowed to affect the case. Now it was potentially a murder, he was very glad Natalie was there. There would be a media frenzy when this got out. And apart from covering his back, and protecting Maeve, Ray was going to need the help.

Maeve wasn't up to the short walk home. She had been standing there, in a daze while the police moved into action. Disconnected from all of their official process, she knew that she was the only one there who knew Anne. Anne, as a person, as her friendly neighbour. They had had such an ordinary normal relationship, how could it end like this?

Natalie was getting ready to go with Steve to break the news to Ray, when Steve offered Maeve a lift on his bike. Steve saw Natalie raise an eyebrow, indicating that she had clocked that Maeve was Steve's potential new love interest. Steve was uncomfortable, but both of them knew that this was not the time to say anything.

Again Maeve was surprised how much she enjoyed holding onto Steve for the short journey back to her house. Again she wasn't ready to address it. So she left Steve and Natalie to do their awful professional task, and went home to tell Marianne and Orla. She would go over to support Ray and relieve Ada as soon as the police left.

Once the news was broken to Ray, Steve made his exit to get back to the crime scene. Natalie stayed to go over procedures, explaining what would happen over the next few days. Ada was the right person to be there, Maeve needed to deal with her own trauma first.

When Steve got back, his police officers were hard at work, they had a banter that spoke of a camaraderie born of years of working together. They were used to dealing with the weekend brawls, the road traffic accidents and student trouble. They were a good team of professional officers and the now accepted police volunteers, they had each other's backs. As Steve arrived, they were setting up the tape cordons, and had officers in place to make sure the public didn't interfere and spoil any evidence. It was a good clean site, no contamination.

Steve thought back to his first case, things were different now. There was definitely more focus on forensics which made for more work at the crime scene and theoretically better outcomes. While the guys were getting on with the work Steve took a moment to think.

Effectively, he had been first on the scene, but if Maeve hadn't been standing there he would have missed the body completely. It wasn't just that he always thought back to his first case, this time there was a notable similarity. Without getting the official autopsy results, he was pretty sure that their first impression was right, and she had died of a broken neck, a quick twist, almost exactly like Susan. What were the odds of that happening twice in Canterbury? Plus the two crime scenes were not far apart, about a 15minutes quick walk, and nine years. But, who would want to hurt an older woman out for an evening stroll? This was no Saturday night alcohol fuelled domestic. This was cold. Was it premeditated?

Scenario planning is part of the job, but jumping to conclusions isn't. That's where good procedures kick in, forcing everyone to follow the right steps and gather information without prejudice, annoyingly it tends to work.

He was checking to see if there could be any natural cause of death, like a heart attack and sudden fall that could have been fatal. There were no obvious tell tale signs. Nothing ordinary seemed to fit. He bent down and looked more closely at the body. Blocking out the sounds around him he focused, imagining he was the victim, how could he have landed like that? He looked again, and thought he saw a slight bruising on the jawbone, just where you might hold the face to give it a quick, sharp twist.

Until the autopsy and the coroner's report confirmed that it was a murder investigation, he would have to start lines of enquiry and following any leads, based on his own suspicions. In medicine they call it the 'golden hour', that time immediately after the emergency which is the most critical in saving the patient. In the police speak it's the 24 hour rule. This was the most critical time to gather evidence, and establish the right lines of enquiry.

The paramedics were waiting with the ambulance, they had to stay until they were given permission to take the body to the morgue. As it happens it was the Hazard Area Response team that had been sent. Steve could hear one of the paramedics talking to the young officer standing guard.

"Canterbury has a surprising number of random deaths, I've had heroin overdoses, a drunken student falling down the stairs landing smack on his head, blood everywhere," Marcus seemed to be enjoying telling his stories.

"One old guy we were called to had been dead a while, he must have fallen badly and twisted his neck, a bit grim by the time we got there. And then there are the homeless ones, who die of exposure sometimes in the woods, and one died right on the High Street, where there must have been people all around him. Not many in or around the university though. And I've never seen a murder before. Of course we normally deal with the living, rescuing people from beaches or cliffs…"

Steve was letting it wash over him, at the same time he was going through a similar litany of untimely deaths, which scenario would lead them to the killer? Were any of them linked?

"Hey, Marcus, you are needed over here, now!" A shout alerted the paramedic to the fact that the body in the crime scene had been recorded, and that the body was now ready to be taken away for autopsy and any relevant forensic investigation. The police constable assigned to accompany the body was waiting impatiently, it had been a long day and he didn't appreciate the idle chatter keeping him from getting home, and he still had to confirm the handover of the body.

Natalie talked Ray through the next steps over and over again. Ada could see the weariness in her face and thought Natalie must be wondering did Ray have early dementia too.

Having picked up on the unintended signs of impatience, Ada interrupted,

"Why don't you leave him now, love? You've been great. And we have all the information we need right now. Ray has your number, if he has any more questions, or thinks of anything useful he knows how to get in touch with you. I think that we all need some time to process this, so I'm saying we should call it a day. Tomorrow we can deal with the next steps."

Ada could see that Ray was grateful, though he still kept coming back to the questions that were uppermost in his mind.

"The funeral, we have to sort that out, there will be an awful lot of people…", he was having trouble taking it in which was clear when he added "Anne will….", as if she was going to appear and take over organising her own funeral, then stopping and putting his head in his hands.

Ada suggested he take a sleeping tablet. Ray said "Right, that's probably a good idea. There will be so much to do….".

Maeve arrived as he was speaking, hearing this as she noticed that Ray looked dazed and Ada had turned white with exhaustion, so said,

"You're right Ada, everyone out. Ray, if it's okay with you, I'm going to stay here tonight, it's not a time to be alone. Thank you officer, thank you Natalie, you have been really helpful".

Within a few minutes Maeve closed the door on them all, and made herself a cup of tea. She had suggested that Ray get ready for bed and she would check in on him. She had taken a spare duvet and was going to wrap herself up on the sofa. When she looked in on Ray he was already out for the count, the sleeping pill had kicked in. But he was restless tossing from side to side mumbling, clearly going over it all in his dreams. She didn't think he would sleep for long. She settled herself, feet up on the couch balancing the mug of hot tea. Putting it down for a minute she stretched out thinking how surprisingly comfortable she was.

The next thing she knew, the mug of stone cold tea was still in front of her, and Ray was standing there washed and dressed, holding out a fresh mug of tea. Her intentions were good, but so much for her vigil.

CHAPTER 20

THE THIRD TIME

Ah yes Kevin, 'Kev', well that was quite a different one. Conspiracy theories are all well and good in a comic book sort of way. Kev liked his conspiracy theories, but he was also a potentially serviceable tool. He had a lot of practical information about the University, and how the systems worked, email traces, back passages for maintenance, and skeleton keys. Yes he had access. If handled correctly, he would pass whatever was needed over, no questions asked.

People who believe in conspiracy theories, who are anti vaccinations, or who swallow 'fake news' as fact, have already been manipulated, but at base they want to be important. They want to be right. They want to be 'in' on the 'secret', so that they can share it, and be the key to information. They are amenable to further manipulation.

How do you do it? With authority. Give them two verifiable facts, then add in your own wild invention, which now seems like a logical progression. Blend verifiable fact with outlandish claims, then shout loudly about rights or the law, and quickly change the subject. It's depressingly easy.

In the beginning, I had fun with Kevin. My game was to see how far I could take him into the land of make-believe. We were searching for 'anti-gravity' powder, which is a bit like a chocolate teapot, but when you combine a secret powder with the Knights Templar, anything is possible. The origins of CABAL are verifiable, and from Dover, so local, but the Catholic House St John's Stone is a modern building, how on earth could they be connected? I had to breathe deeply to suppress the laughter. I loved to hear him spread these new facts to others, making-up his own weird rationale to explain the unexplainable. Delightful.

After a while, his smell began to get to me. I admit I am fastidious. A sharp dresser, if I say so myself, and I like to smell fresh. To put it bluntly, Kev was dirty. That kind of dirt where the grime on his shirt collars would never wash off. The reek of stale cigarettes would waft in front of him to announce his arrival. This bothered me, it began to disgust me. His conversation became tedious, he was a bore, but more importantly, he had begun to link me with missing people. One day I decided that I had had enough, I didn't need him anymore, it was time.

The plan for his death was meticulous. I made it look like one of those domestic accidents. As though he had tripped on the stairs and fallen, simple and clean. His neck was surprisingly fragile. I thought I might have twisted it a bit too far, in the end it looked perfect. I placed his head in such a way on the step you could see that with his gross weight landing on his face, that would have been sufficient to have twisted it. I even gave evidence as the last person to have seen him.

CHAPTER 21

TRYING FOR NORMAL

Marianne and Orla had taken over looking after Ada. Ada was confidently optimistic that she was back to better than normal, and could do anything she wanted to, but it was clear to everyone else, that she tired easily. Ada was thoroughly enjoying having young people around her, and wasn't sure if it was all the love and attention, or the new stents, but she was feeling a million dollars. That morning, Marianne had found the homemade brown bread in the freezer, made toast and coffee, plus of course Barry's tea for Ada. Orla added her own favourite raspberry jam from the garden. There were plenty of times when both Orla and Marianne could irritate each other, but in a crisis they knew how to pull together.

Ada was presiding over the breakfast table, on her second cup of tea, when with a twinkle in her eye said,

"So Orla, what's all this 'eco warrior' business I am hearing about, should I be afraid? I don't want my beautiful granddaughter in combats looking like a para!"

Orla was building up her self righteous indignation when she twigged that Ada was making fun of her, still with a sniff she said

"It's all right for you, your generation, and Mum's, have been heating your houses with our future!"

Nice turn of phrase thought Marianne, who was always more thoughtful and less likely to have an outburst, but admiring of Orla's chutzpah.

Next door, Maeve was doing a re-cap with Ray, and making plans for the day. Ray was still like a startled rabbit caught in headlights, without saying anything directly, he was leaning on Maeve to tell him what to do next. Natalie had already explained the technical processes a few times the night before. As she left the printed guidance leaflet with Ray, she had said

"No-one takes it all in at first. The shock, wipes your mind of everything other than that your loved one is dead. You need something in black and white to read, and reread later on, even then, you only take it in a bit at a time." She had been more specific when she said

"We will need you, Ray, to come and officially identify the body in the morning. An officer will call you to arrange a time with the coroner's office in Maidstone. The body will be much nearer, in the morgue in the hospital in Canterbury. A post mortem will take place, and then the coroner's office will let you know when the body can be removed to the funeral directors. After that you can set the date for the funeral. I expect it will take a few days because of the circumstances."

Natalie had also gone through the other aspects he might want to prepare for, including the possibility of media interest. Had it been a search, the police would have encouraged media interest, now they wanted to assess all the information they had before opening the floodgates. So, fingers crossed, they should have a day or two before the local reporters found out.

Ray may not have taken it all in, but a funeral was something he knew about. Handling the press was not. He was very glad that Maeve and Ada were there to help him. His daughter Ruth was flying back from Egypt, and should arrive sometime during the day but definitely by nightfall. He was in the middle of telling Maeve the plans that he and Anne had made to be cremated, when the coroner rang. They decided that it was best not to leave the house empty in case anyone called. As it was mostly going to be a time to rest, they asked Ada to mind the house, or more likely 'phone sit'. She was happily settled in with her fresh pot of tea, as Maeve drove Ray the ten minutes over to the hospital.

"We shouldn't be long, and you should be taking it easy too. I must say you are looking great," Maeve was trying to strike a balance between her previous almost abrupt way of talking to her mother and her newfound 'sharing' which was a bit gushy and could sound insincere if she wasn't careful. Ada didn't seem to mind,

"Oh God! I'm fine. Don't rush back for me."

Ray was struggling to keep himself together, so was concentrating on dealing with practical things one at a time. Maeve listened as he ran through the list in the car,

" We have to identify the body. We know that Ruth is arriving today, but not the exact time. Traffic from Heathrow will be bad if she hit's rush hour. Should I go and pick her up?"

"No, Ruth is fine, she has already organised a car to pick her up. Do you remember, she said she wanted to try and sleep in the car?" Maeve was firm, he was in no state to drive, but she knew he was anxious to be doing the right thing.

Back on his list,

"Must check there are clean sheets on the bed. Need to get some fresh milk."

He was almost talking to himself. Maeve had a strong sense that he still hadn't taken in that Anne wasn't coming back, and that all this was so that he could tell Anne what he had done while she was out.

Not long after they left the house, the doorbell rang. Must have left the keys or something, Ada thought, as she got up to answer it. She opened the door, with a 'what is it now' attitude when her jaw dropped. Standing outside was Simon Evans, the TV reporter for BBC South East. Ada knew him as a pushy young man, a reporter who would walk over anyone, twist any facts, to get a good story. Equally he knew Ada, as the crank 'mystic medium' who would talk to your dead relatives for a fee. In fact he had done a feature on the 'fake psychics of Kent', and as Ada was the most striking looking, half the footage was of her at her most flamboyant. In reality, it had done Ada no harm, and ultimately she got a lot of new clients from the attention, but it was a damning piece. He didn't know that she had benefited from it, so she certainly wasn't going to tell him now.

Simon had already set up his ridiculously small iPhone on a tripod and was filming. He had his interview clothes on, a standard white shirt and tie, with a sports jacket, and had a microphone already pointed towards Ada. Although Simon was clearly taken aback at seeing Ada, he did a quick rethink and went on seamlessly.

"Ada McPhilips, infamous spirit medium at the house of the deceased, what can you tell us about this tragic case?"

Simon had had a tip off from a friend, who was a new volunteer in the police force. He was still so excited about his important role, that he forgot Simon was a news reporter, and that as a member of the police force, albeit unpaid, he should have kept his mouth shut. A late night beer had turned into a scoop for Simon.

Simon knew that he was on thin ice, nothing had been confirmed. The name of the deceased was not yet in the public domain, but he liked a good story and a murder could get him national syndication. At his age he needed to be noticed to move up the ladder, this exposure was just perfect. If he could get his interview now, before any other journalists arrived, he could edit it and hold the piece till he got the all clear. If he was lucky he could have it on this evening's news before anyone else even got their interview. And a medium was going to be the icing on the cake. Never mind the old saying 'if it bleeds it leads' he had a much better headline 'The Dead are Helping the Police'.

Ada knew this wasn't about her, but she had not been communing with the other side since her heart attack, which was a piece of information that she didn't want to share. She was convinced this was only a temporary situation, and that as soon as she recovered, well, she would recover her gift too, wouldn't she? As a result she was on the defensive on two counts. How to handle this? It was later that Ada wondered how Simon had arrived on the scene so quickly, was he involved somehow? She wouldn't put anything past him. For now Ada decided that confidence was the right attitude, she would be what she was, a concerned neighbour, who would help in any way they could. That sounded right in her own head.

But it didn't end up that way. Somehow she managed to talk about herself, and her string of happy clients too. Old habits die hard, and Ada was used to seeking publicity for her work. She ended up turning it into a bit of more a promo than she intended, leaving her with an uneasy feeling that she might not have done the right thing.

By the time they got back from the hospital it was already mid morning, and both Maeve and Ray were flagging. It had been gruelling. Anne had looked peaceful, almost asleep. But Ray had taken it very badly. They had had to wait for the same PC, who had accompanied Anne last night, to be there, to identify the body, which had given them some time. Ray needed it. He needed to say his 'goodbyes'.

Maeve had been right, up till then, he really thought that she would be back any minute. Now he was faced with the fact, she was dead, it was definite, final. Maeve gave him some time, then to help him get through the day she kept him focused on the things to be done, knowing that the grieving process wouldn't really start until after the funeral.

Years ago, she had listened to Ada talking about death and grieving with her clients, who often came out with the same kind of comments and reflections. 'It's the empty place at the table; the voice messages that you don't want to delete; that there's nothing to look forward to; it's all in the past now.' Maeve also knew that it does get better as time goes on, or you come to an accommodation with the situation, but it takes time, a lot more time than you think. Right now, concentrating on the business of the day, gets you through the next hour, the next day, and so on. She knew that most of this would be a blur for Ray, something he wouldn't want to remember. She knew that she just had to be there for him, tissues at the ready.

Steve had left a message. 'The police needed to do a formal interview with Ray, and also with Maeve. As soon as they were up to it could they come down to the station?'

Ada made them some toast and coffee to give them some strength before facing the police. They both looked drawn, and Ray sat still making comments from time to time to no one in particular.

"..She just went out for a walk....Why would someone want to hurt her?..."

Ada didn't manage to find the right time to tell them about the BBC. It would do as soon as they got back, wouldn't it? No rush yet.

The interviews at the police station took a lot longer than Maeve was expecting. The whole process was disconcertingly professional. This wasn't her friend Steve, this was business.

There were two police officers in the interview room, and as the tape recorder was switched on Steve said,

" for the record this is Detective Inspector Stephen Maguire with Family Liaison Officer, Constable Natalie Gosby, interviewing Maeve McPhillips.

You have a right to silence.

Whatever you say can be used against you in a criminal case in court.

If you don't mention something now which you mention later a court might ask why you didn't mention it at the first opportunity".

This was an interview under caution.

It was at about this point, that it registered with Maeve, that helping the police could be misinterpreted as being a suspect. Of course, as she thought about it, without anyone else under suspicion the first people to eliminate, or suspect, of committing the crime, are the partner, (as in the case of domestic abuse), or the person who found the body. Given that this person might also be the last person to see the victim alive, that put her in a precarious position.

This was a shock. Shouldn't she have a lawyer present? This not being Maeve's world, random thoughts were running through her head, and she was leaning on vaguely remembered police procedural TV shows. Then the Guildford Four, and the Birmingham Six, popped into her mind. From the news coverage of them, she did recall that the English legal system is an adversarial system. You may be innocent until proven guilty, but the role of the police is to provide the necessary evidence to the Crown Prosecution Service to convict the guilty. She felt very uncomfortable. Whatever her relationship with Steve might have been, at this moment in time, they were literally on opposite sides of the table. Even though she was trembling, she knew she would regret it if she didn't take action right now,

"I think I need a lawyer present." And with that, everything stopped,

"Interview terminated at 1.05pm."

Once they were out of the interview room, Steve tried to explain that this was just normal police procedure, that it might have been an accident, or a serious crime which looked like murder. Maeve stopped him with

"I'm sure that's what they said to the Guildford Four. So I think 'better safe than sorry' don't you? And you are right, procedures are there to be followed and I should have a lawyer with me. And Ray should too. Do you have a list of appropriate lawyers that do it pro-bono, or for legal aid?"

Steve was getting irritated,

"We don't think either of you had anything to do with it, but if we don't do everything by the book we can't clear you either." With that they stopped talking to each other.

The sourcing of legal representation was always going to slow things down, which is why Steve had tried to get through this without one. Maeve popped out to get sandwiches for Ray and herself, the police had given them tea. Steve was on his phone pacing with frustration. He needed to be out pursuing all lines up at the University, not wasting time in the station, but equally, he knew he had to do the interviews.

By the time Maeve and Ray had had their meeting with the lawyer, and finally got through the interviews, this time with the lawyer present, it was late afternoon. Nothing strange or startling emerged, but Maeve felt that she had done the right thing, even though the results looked like she had made a fuss over nothing. She certainly didn't make any friends at the station.

As they were leaving, Ada sent a text saying that Ray's daughter Ruth had arrived and that she had sorted food for supper, did they have any idea how long they would be?

. . .

At Ray's house, Ada had left Ruth sorting herself out, and had gone back to Maeve's, checked what was in the fridge and put on some roast chicken and new potatoes, thinking it would do. Nothing fancy, and no one was likely to notice anyway. She was sufficiently distracted, that she didn't think to tell anyone about Simon's early morning visit. and that he had been filming it.

Ruth and Ray came over to eat what Ada had prepared at Maeve's, and it did them all good, they could sit in comfortable silence with no pressure to be anything other than themselves. Hot food appeared on the table, in a warm and friendly atmosphere. Marianne and Orla had known Ruth since they were little girls, Ruth was the one they both looked up to. So there was no awkwardness. No need to prepare a face, they were all in this together. As a result none of them saw the item on TV.

That night, they all needed sleep, and so it was that their phones were on silent too.

Regardless of whether they had seen the news item or not, none of them could have been prepared for what happened next.

CHAPTER 22

THE 'BUST-UP'!

Marianne had one priority, which was to focus on studying for the exams. Up till now she had kept herself together, and life had been more or less manageable. Marianne had always been the quiet one, the strong one. She could do anything, once she had the time to mentally prepare for it. Surprises of any kind however, were not appreciated.

Before all of this upheaval, she had been thinking that the May bank holiday weekend would probably be the last time she could take a break before the exams. Maeve had suggested that she should take a short break, which at the time, she poo-poo-ed, but now, Marianne was considering that maybe Maeve was right. In spite of the emotional upset, and arrival of Ada, and the terrible dramas next door, she was still on top of her revision, just.

Her schedule had worked out pretty well, and she had built in some extra 'just-in-case' time. She was confident that she could take a long weekend off. She wanted to scoot over to Arras and see her other family.

She had a great relationship with her Dad, Pascal, and although she never liked to say it to Maeve, she also really enjoyed her stepmother Marie-Odile, who was more like a friend than a parent. But the kids were the real reason she wanted to go. They loved her. They demanded her full attention, stories, shopping, playing games. It was the best way to take her mind off things, and that would give her a proper rest. Right now she needed something to give her that sense of calm normality, not this crazy phase where everyone was rocking her world. She needed time to reset, to get her head straight, ready for the final push.

Thinking it through Marianne convinced herself, if she was going to do it, today was the right time. It would be fine. She thought that Orla was better than her in situations like this, and really Mum could do with one less to look after.

For once in her life Marianne decided to just act. She took her backpack, with enough stuff for a short stay. She had her phone, so they could contact her, and she left a note in the middle of the floor, on the mat by the front door. She didn't want to get into a face to face explanation, it would be better in a note. As she left the house, she noticed a large number of cars arriving and people milling around. She guessed it had something to do with Anne, which confirmed to her that this really was a good time to get out.

Ruth was exhausted from the travel, and Ray had taken another sleeping pill so he was flat out. Maeve had collapsed into her own bed. Ada had ear plugs in, her eye mask on, and was oblivious to the world. So it was Orla feeding the cat and getting ready for school who saw it first.

By this time, the whole street was blocked off with cars, vans and outside broadcast units, parked anywhere, and everywhere. They were on the road, in the road, and all over peoples gardens. There were television reporters each talking to their own camera crews and each with a view of Ray's house. It seemed that the day before had been a quiet news day, globally. Simon's report of a spirit medium helping the police to solve a crime, potentially a murder, was just the sort of gossipy story that people all over the world love, so it had spread like wildfire. Simon was fighting to keep his place near the house, but it didn't matter to him, he had already had the scoop. Plus he had the old footage of Ada, which he could use again and again. There were crews from everywhere, ITV, BBC, Sky, and internationally too, from CNN, from Japanese TV, Russian TV and on and on.

Orla ran up the stairs, and woke Maeve, while precariously checking the internet on her laptop. By the time Maeve was awake, Orla had the full story. Simon's piece along with images of Ada, looking the very picture of a glamorous medium, to a sound bite of 'I help the dead to tell their story'. This was intercut with Simon talking outside the house just as Ada, the helpful neighbour, opened the door. It was all over the internet, it was everywhere! Simon had been very clever, and had cut together a great story. Ada's extra promotional comments combined with Simon's sharp edit really made it sound as though she was here to solve the crime, most of which was Simon's speculation, but until someone spilled the beans it was all anyone had to go on.

"Christ Mum! What have you done! How could you!" Maeve was too upset to hold back. She shook Ada awake,

"What, darling, I'm still asleep, I can't hear a thing with the earplugs in, aren't they great.."Ada trailed off as by this stage Maeve had shoved the laptop in front of her showing the news clip.

"When were you going to tell us? Or was this just another opportunity for you to be the great 'I am', the one taking centre stage? It's been like that all my life and I thought we could get beyond it. Clearly not. It's more important that the great Ada, the spirit medium, gets the publicity. Christ sake mother, Anne is dead! This could tip Ray over into a full on breakdown. Some friend you are."

Maeve didn't draw breath and she wasn't going to listen to any 'excuses' Ada might have. Maeve had thrown on some clothes and was hopping over the back wall to get into next door, hopefully before Ray and Ruth saw the frenzy outside the front of the house.

Ada shouted after her,

"I didn't do anything, I swear it, on my dying mother's grave I swear it!."

Maeve didn't reply, she didn't believe it, if it really was a mistake wouldn't Ada have told them about it last night? How on earth was she going to apologise to Ray and Ruth!

Ada was beside herself, crying, as she rocked back and forth,

"That bastard! I didn't say anything much, he made most of it up."

Orla was trying to comfort her, rubbing her back saying,

"It'll be fine, when she calms down Mum'll be fine, you'll see" but Ada knew different. They had unresolved issues, secrets that Orla knew nothing about which meant that Maeve might never speak to her again, as this realisation dawned on Ada, another wave of tears broke, she was incoherent and unconsolable.

Maeve had managed to sneak into the house without any of the reporters seeing her. She would never forgive Ada, but that was for another time, right now she needed to warn Ruth and Ray. She managed to wake them up, make tea, and get them into the kitchen before they realised what was outside the house. She had brought her laptop and just showed them the news clip. Ray was still groggy and couldn't take it in. Luckily Ruth was in PR, so she realised what had happened probably even better than Maeve. Maeve explained that there were tens of news crews camped outside in their normally empty Close.

Ruth turned into her professional persona,

"Right, I am going to sneak into the living room and close the curtains. Whatever you do, nobody is to answer the door. Maeve, can you pull down the blinds in the kitchen and the shutters in the breakfast room. But don't look out the windows, we have to assume that they all have telephoto lenses. Once we have shut down the house, I suggest that Dad and I get showered and dressed and by then I will have come up with a press statement. Oh, and Maeve, can you call your policeman friend? I think we should let them know what's happening and make sure that our stories are along the same lines."

Maeve was so relieved that she could have kissed her. She found it hard to imagine that this was the same Ruth who when she left home, was little older than Marianne just off to college. Ruth had always been bright as a button, and had been happy to play with Marianne and Orla. She had no strong ambition for herself, and she never, ever wanted to be the centre of attention. Yet here she was, taking it all in her stride. Maybe having a drama to sort that was more like her work, was giving her a way to put off facing that Anne was gone.

Meanwhile, Ada had recovered enough to get ready for the day, drink her tea and even nibble a slice of toast. Orla had decided that this wasn't a day for school so was doing whatever she could for Ada. She was glad that Marianne must have gone to school early for some extra study and missed it all. Orla knew that if she were here, Marianne would try to make her go to school. So this was easier.

With more spirit than she has shown since she woke up, Ada made a decision,

" Okay, I've got it. This is what we will do. Orla, you are going to help me pack. We are going to get a taxi to Sandgate, I am going home. You are going to come with me. It's Friday so you can come and stay for the weekend. You can be my nurse and make sure I don't have another heart attack! That way we can leave Maeve some space. Maybe by Monday she will be ready to talk to me."

Ada sat, while, in a flurry of activity, Orla tidied the breakfast things, packed both bags and ordered a taxi. They didn't think anymore about Marianne, because she would be in class by now. She was probably the best one to handle Maeve at the moment anyway, especially if Ada was out of the way.

The taxi arrived, parking a distance away from the house because the news crews were in the way, rather than anybody's good planning. By the look of them, the news teams were getting settled in.

Scarf over her head and dark glasses on, Ada had 'borrowed' Maeve's navy blue patched Barbour jacket. She was trying to look more like an ordinary local, or at least less conspicuous than her own gold lame shower proof cloak. In the rush to leave the house as discreetly as possible, neither Ada nor Orla, had noticed the sheet of paper in the middle of their 'welcome' doormat. They had just shoo-ed the cat, who was sitting on it, out of the way. As they shut the door a gust of wind picked up the sheet of paper and blew it behind the old fashioned coat stand. It was just visible, with a corner peeping out, and Marianne's writing was recognisable, 'Mum, I have ….'

CHAPTER 23

MISSING

Having got the house dark, by creeping around on hands and knees, closing curtains, shutter or blinds without being seen, Maeve was feeling like she had somehow landed in the middle of an American thriller, a bit like Will Smith in 'Enemy of the State'.

She could hear the shower going upstairs, and was facing the bit she really didn't want to do. But she would rather make this call now, when there was no one around, she really didn't want anyone eavesdropping. She wasn't sure how she felt about Steve, and hadn't had the time to decide if he really had been 'just doing his job' in a way that would clear her and Ray, or not. Nothing for it, she was going to have to call him, right now before showers were finished, or it would get even more awkward.

Steve wasn't keen on talking to Maeve either. What had she been playing at? Wasn't it clear that he found her attractive? That meant he had to be extra cautious, always have a witness present, always record any important conversation as a statement. Maybe she really wasn't aware, maybe it did look like she was a suspect. Unconsciously, maybe he did think she might have done it, did he? No! That was ridiculous. He had seen how she looked when she had found the body. Was there a sliver of doubt? Okay, maybe he could see how it might have appeared to Maeve. He was still right to have done what he did, but maybe she had a point, he had made her a suspect without explaining the process. Maybe he had done it because he hadn't decided what kind of relationship he wanted with Maeve. He hadn't had any time to reflect on it either, when Maeve called.

Steve had also missed the evening news, so it caught him on the hop too.

"Oh God!"

This was just what he didn't need. A media frenzy.

"What was your mother thinking of? A medium helping with police enquiries! Shit! I have to sort things here immediately, I'll call you back, don't do anything until we have spoken."

With that he hung up and warned the desk sergeant. Too late. They had already been inundated with calls, and had been fending them off with a 'the police do not work with psychics, no further comment' set of responses.

Once Ada and Orla had set off for Sandgate, Ada started making plans,

"This is going to be like going into hiding."

Orla was never one to let an inaccuracy go so she cheerfully corrected,

"It's not 'like' going into hiding, you *are* going into hiding! And I am acting as your 'handler', as well as your minder." That was a lot worse than Ada liked the sound of.

By the time Steve called Maeve, they had both had a moment to think, maybe it wasn't completely the other one's fault, but still, there were wounded egos on both sides. They were civil rather than warm. Meanwhile Ruth had gone through her statement and had a list of questions. She wanted to know if the police had any lines of enquiry, or if she should add in anything specific like 'if anyone has any information they should call….', or should they organise a joint press conference?

Maeve handed the phone over to Ruth. As she did so she thought, what am I doing in the middle of this, how did I get here? Ruth and Steve decided that given the unusual level of media interest, they should hold a joint press conference. They could both state that this had nothing to do with any psychics, the reporter had been completely mistaken, Ada was a friend and neighbour, nothing more. They would hold it in town to draw the media away from the house, while Maeve, and in particular Ada, would hide next door.

Having already arrived in Sandgate, Orla was enjoying her position of power.

"We need supplies and you can't go out, both because you need the rest, and because everyone knows you, but they think you are in Canterbury. So don't put your nose outside the door. I'm going to go to the East Yard, to the Docker Brewery and Bakehouse in the harbour over in Folkestone. I want to get the best sourdough ever, have you tried it yet? I'll get some fresh fish from Trawlers too, and I was thinking we should get a few beers, what do you say?"

Orla skirted the alcohol question with,

"It's okay, I'm pescatarian, I can eat fish, and I can use your card if I tap it."

Ada didn't feel that she could object, she wasn't allowed to drive yet anyway. The girls had kept two bikes in her house for years, so that they could go on their own excursions anytime they were over. Taking the credit card that Ada held out as she nodded her assent, Orla picked out Marianne's bike, because it was an old fashioned upright model, with a wicker basket on the front, which would be great for the shopping.

. . .

Back in Canterbury, Maeve had waited 'till Ruth went out the front door then, as she slipped out the back unseen, she could just hear Ruth saying,

"We appreciate your support at this difficult time for our family….",

Over her shoulder, she glimpsed the media surging around Ruth as she turned back, and hopped over the fence, home. She had steeled herself to face Ada, and was stunned to find the house empty, and all of Ada's stuff gone too.

That morning as Marianne had carefully placed her note explaining where she was going and closed the door quietly behind her, she had felt her heart lift. She thought a note was the best way to break the news. She didn't want anyone to stop her, nor did she want to disturb or upset her Mum. This way, by the time Maeve read it, she would probably have arrived safely in France, and then Maeve couldn't be too upset. Anyway she could call when she was on the train. She felt for her phone which was comforting, her security blanket.

This was a completely controlled adventure, and it was just for her. It wasn't until she was walking to the train station that she realised how much the recent stress and tension surrounding her Mum, Ada, Orla and now Anne, had affected her. The exams were bad enough, but the rest was in a whole different league. She thought, if I shut it all out for the weekend, take some time doing ordinary things with people I love, then I will be fresh and ready to take on the next phase of revision, and of life.

School had already been winding down and putting more emphasis on self study timetables, so missing a day wasn't a problem. As she walked, she called her friend Rachael, and told her that she wasn't feeling great so was going to stay home today. Marianne thought that there was no point in getting anyone else into trouble for lying. Rachael would simply relay the message. Marianne felt a bit guilty at Rachael's concerned 'are you alright'? Should I come over?'

But knew that this was the best way not to land Rachael in trouble if it ever came out that she had taken the day off. Marianne never took time out of school, so no one would doubt her. Job done.

It was only as she switched her phone off and put it in her bag that she noticed her battery charge was almost zero and thought. She rummaged in her bag but after a few moments, 'Shit! Ada must have 'borrowed' my charger!'

Ada was always generous with her possessions, and it didn't seem to occur to her that 'borrowing' things without people's permission could be really annoying. Letting the stress go, Marianne thought 'never mind'. It wasn't a serious problem, she had left a note, and could call from Dad's to make doubly sure. Mum had other things to deal with so wouldn't notice till this evening anyway.

Marianne could now concentrate on enjoying the day. She was in no rush. She planned it as she walked, she would take the train to Ashford, and catch the next Eurostar to Calais, maybe wander around the market in Calais. Get her favourite ham and cheese baguette and a grand cafe creme, watch the world go by for a while. Then take the local train to Arras, in time to walk over and meet Dad at the Salon. Easy.

It was after lunch before Ada remembered that she hadn't told Maeve where she was, nor that Orla was with her. 'Dammit!' She looked at her phone which she had left on silent from the night before. Of course there were missed calls from Maeve, four to be precise, one an hour, and the text, 'where the f**k are you?' Not surprising really, if she were in Maeve's shoes she'd be mad too.

Thinking of the best way to handle it, Ada decided to text first, then Maeve could call her whenever she was ready, 'Hello love, so, so, sorry about the TV, thought it best to get out of your hair. Took Orla with me. At home now. All okay here. Call when you want to xxxxx'. She said a silent prayer as she pressed send.

. . .

Anger doesn't really describe what Maeve was feeling, she was beside herself with rage, 'that woman, only ever thinks of herself. Never a thought for others. Actually that's not true. Plenty of time for others, just none for me. She never had time for me.' The anger mixed with the sadness, and self pity that Maeve could fall into when she thought about Ada. Looking at it now she knew that it was a lack of affection, a lack of love. Ada had never really loved her, she thought. Not in the way Maeve loved Marianne and Orla.

Maeve had brought her children up in a household full of affection, full of hugs and kisses, full of laughter. A house where people had time for the children, and brought them into the conversation. Thinking back on her own childhood she remembered it as lonely. Ada, drifting around, and her father identifying Maeve as a nuisance, a problem to be managed. Maeve was always a disappointment to him, irrationally everything that went wrong was her fault. Maeve thought it was probably because she wasn't a boy, but there seemed more to it than that. Maeve never understood what made her father so dismissive, and frequently downright mean to her. Nor why Ada never seemed to take her side.

All of the emotions that Maeve had been going through the last few days caught up with her, and she cried. Cried for her lost childhood, cried that she couldn't reconnect with Ada, maybe she could never fully feel loved by Ada, cried for what she hadn't managed to do.

Was she trying for the impossible? She felt that she had failed on every count. She hadn't found Anne in time, even though she had had the warning. At a certain point she had nothing left, she had cried herself out. She sat in the emptiness for a few minutes, then the other Maeve took over, telling herself to have something to eat, have a cup of tea, think things through again. It will all work out.

Feeling restored, she was about to tidy up when Ruth called, and explained

"The press fiasco wasn't completely Ada's fault. Ada had never actually mentioned helping the police, that was all fabrication on behalf of the journalist. Of course, the fact that Ada was a medium did mean, anyone who knew that, could put two and two together, but Ada didn't do it on purpose. I wouldn't want you to blame her. The media do know how to make a good story. "

By the time she came off the call Maeve was up to date. The police were starting their lines of enquiry, and had used the conference to call for any witnesses. Things were progressing. Also, they had talked things over and had decided to have the funeral a week today, which was surely long enough for the autopsy, and would also give Ruth's brother time to get to Canterbury from Australia.

Maeve phoned Ada, now in a much better place. They made a sort of peace. It was still out of order for Ada to take Orla out of school like that, but maybe this wasn't the time to push it. So Maeve decided that a nice quiet evening with Marianne was just what she needed. As she reflected on the last week, it was probably just what Marianne needed too, a bit of normality. She would bake one of the family favourites, a cheese pie, and serve it with a green salad with avocado and asparagus, dressed with Ottolenghi's simple olive oil, garlic and lemon juice dressing, perfect.

Maeve made the pastry, put it in the fridge and thought, there's enough time to stretch my legs before I have to get the pie in the oven. Throwing on her denim jacket, she went towards town, not keen on going up to the University just yet. She ended up crossing Beverly Meadow, and there waiting for her was Susan who addressed her with,

"Glad you came by, I am sorry about that lady, she is a nice lady. But you need to know that it is not over. You must find the killer or the price you pay will be too high."

After this cryptic comment, not waiting for a reply, Susan had disappeared.

CHAPTER 24
THE FOURTH TIME

Starting to contemplate a murder gives me a frisson of excitement. Identifying someone I have seen, following them as they go about their business adds to it. Then being clever, working out how to leave no traces, throwing any potential detectives off the scent, that feels satisfying too. I like to create a good story, I know how to put the pieces together to make a good story. They don't normally recruit for intelligence, I should hope that I could outwit them. From experience I know that I can. I can be there, watch them and laugh inside. Cat and mouse.

I was beginning to feel the need rise up in me again. The need for that excitement and release. Planning is good, but I can also see opportunities that just present themselves to me, and know how to use them to my best advantage. Isolated walkers, those alone, are good ones to notice when they appear. Sometimes you have to go with the flow. Life throws things at you and you have to just recognise the opportunities when they are in front of you.

The need is growing stronger. In the way drug addicts talk about needing more, I do too.

CHAPTER 25

MORE THAN ONE?

By mid afternoon Marianne had enjoyed her mooch around Calais, revelling in her favourite bits of France, had taken the local train, changed at St Omer, and arrived in Arras.

She was walking from the station down to the Rue Meaulens, breathing in memories and putting the recent stress behind her. Through the Place des Heros, toward the town hall where the giants are kept between festivals. Orla and Marianne had been part of the group to make 'the baby', which was the first addition in a generation to the ten foot tall giant family.

She walked on, taking a detour via her primary school, where as a four year old she had excelled at dance. Her big moment being to lead the class routine at the annual kermesse, the school fete. It all seemed so long ago, strange and yet familiar. She caught the smell of beer from the obligatory Irish Pub, and more pleasantly the lingering smell of this morning's baguettes from the boulangerie. As she passed, she eavesdropped into the chatter in french as people went about their business.

The workday was coming to a close and the weekend was beginning. It was liberating, it was the break she needed. She walked beyond her father's barber's salon, because she could see him with a client through the window. Stopping at the Frite van, parked on the wide verge of the bridge by the Jardin Minelle overlooking the canal basin. There were a few park benches to sit on, and admire the geometric concrete plant holders full of colourful tulips, wallflowers and pansies. With the water in the background, it was a nice spot to sit and wait.

As she sat, Marianne looked under the old stone arches, taking in the full height plate glass that had been used to form the walls of the shop front through which she could see her Dad working.

He was smiling, taking time with the customer, chatting as if it was no effort, yet he was totally focused on doing a meticulous job. She could imagine the conversation. As a little girl, when she could, she would dress up in a white overall that was much too big for her, and take charge of sweeping up the hair. Her father had taught her how to be 'professional', and take pride in doing a job properly. She would hold the tall brush, which was much bigger than her, standing to attention, waiting till she got the imperceptible nod. Then she would move in, and neatly gather the fallen hair in a pile, taking it away in time for her Dad to move back into place with the mirror, and show the client the finished result. She was very serious, the regulars loved to see her there, sometimes clients would bring her sweets, which she always shared. Her father had told her how to be fair, and share your tips, so she did. Marianne found herself smiling at her own memories.

Then she noticed Marie-Odile arriving with the children, they hadn't seen her. As they entered the salon they swarmed over Pascal, and he, happy with the interruption kissed them. Clearly they had come to pick him up. She looked at the car which Marie-Odile had left parked on the double yellow lines with hazard lights flashing. It was packed full of stuff for the beach. Marianne hadn't told them that she was coming, and it hadn't occurred to her till this instant, that they might have plans for the weekend.

. . .

Back at home, food prepared, glass of wine in hand, it was Friday after all. Maeve had caught up with herself and looked at the time thinking 'Actually, where is Marianne, she is normally home from school long before now?' She phoned Ada. As the phone rang her level of irritation rose, which she was finding hard to keep under control, thinking that it would have been much easier to get all of this sorted earlier.

Her tone betrayed her thoughts,

"So is Marianne with you too?"

Ada was really keen to make sure that there were no misunderstandings this time,

"No, love, I haven't seen her since first thing this morning. Actually I didn't even hear her leaving for school."

Ada, now shouting at her end,

"Orla, dear, did you hear Marianne leave this morning? No, you didn't either… Maeve, you still there? Maybe she went to have a coffee with her friends in town before coming home..?" Maeve had already hung up.

Within a few minutes Maeve had established that Marianne had not gone to school. That, according to her friend Rachael, she might be ill, and that no one had in fact seen her since about 8am this morning. Maeve left numerous messages on Marianne's phone, but it was either out of range, switched off, or had run out of batteries. She knew that there was enough credit on the phone, so it wasn't that.

She called Steve.

He was off duty but came around anyway. Most of the press had left for the day, but there were a few lingering. The mess would take some clean-up. They had parked everywhere, torn up the grass between the footpath and the road, trampled on garden flowers and left any number of takeaway coffee cups and sandwich wrappers. Steve didn't think that the remaining few would stay long, nor that they would be interested in him. He didn't look like a policeman, just an ordinary bloke on a motorbike and with the helmet they wouldn't look twice.

Steve had had another gruelling day, the impromptu press conference had taken time that he needed to spend elsewhere.

When he arrived, Maeve was agitated and needed something to do as she talked, so automatically fed him. He was happy to enjoy some good food, as she talked through everything she knew so far. Between mouthfuls Steve explained that they wouldn't start a search for 48 hours or longer, because she was fit and healthy and they had no reason to suspect anything bad had happened. Young people often 'disappear' and really have gone to visit friends. Plus he had already taken the details, which is all that they would do down at the station. Anne's case became urgent when they realised that she had dementia.

Actually, earlier in the day, at the station, his colleague had had a report of another missing person. It wasn't Steve's case, but he had begun to wonder if there might be a link with Anne's death, which had now been classed as murder. He decided not to mention it to Maeve just yet, as it was most likely to upset her even more. He thought the case was a young lad that hadn't shown up as a replacement teacher, and wasn't to be found, could they be linked?

Now Maeve couldn't sit still,

"Let's walk her school route, just in case." He suggested.

It wasn't likely that they would be able to see anything in the dark, but they took a torch, and it was good to be in the fresh air. Just in case Marianne arrived before they got back, Maeve left a huge note on the doormat telling Marianne to call her ASAP. As they walked, Steve realised that it was probably best that he go through some of the situations that they had to face on a reasonably regular basis, and let Maeve work out which one might apply.

"Young people are both predictable and unpredictable, what do we know? It was a school day and she's a good student, so either she was ill, or she wanted a day off. If she was ill where would she go?"

They both thought that home was likely, but if she had come home and found the press where might she go then? Or might she be in hospital? A quick call from her mobile solved that one.

Marianne was not at the hospital.

"Does she have a current boyfriend? Would she tell you if she did?", Steve had thought that a weekend off for two young people might be a realistic option. Maeve was firm on that one,

"Nope, she did have one but she decided that he was just boring and that if she wasn't studying she would rather read a book!", which Maeve had agreed was a perfectly valid life choice.

Steve was going through his mental checklist,

"Any close relatives? Other than Ada."

At this Maeve got excited,

"Relatives! I should have thought about that before. Christ. Her father. Pascal lives in France, the girls have often gone over on their own, it's not far, just the other side of the Channel."

She was dialling as she spoke. Pascal answered and she could hear Marie-Odile trying to keep the children quiet in the background,

"Sorry, we are getting ready, on our way to the coast to Le Touquet, we are all going parasailing this time,..."

Maeve interrupted the happy chatter abruptly,

"Have you seen Marianne? She is missing."

Pascal nearly dropped the phone,

"She's not here. But this is totally bizarre, I was just finishing up with the last client and I thought I could feel her nearby. I was thinking I should call. Then the kids arrived and I forgot, and now this. Weird. Okay, we go to Le Touquet. I can leave the kids with Marie-Odile and some friends there. I am coming over to Canterbury, I will be there in the morning."

For a moment Maeve felt relieved then, she ran through the full implications of having Pascal stressing too.

"No! We're just panicking, what can you do here? If we are all in one place we can't cover as many bases. Much better that you are there, in case she is coming to you! Check your home before you go, then keep your phone with you. That way if we hear anything whichever one of us is closer can go to her."

Pascal was silent as he considered this option,

"That sounds like a good plan, we must call each other if we hear anything at all, or even think of something that might be useful…"

He petered out a bit deflated but at the same time reassured, brains rather than heart had kicked in, less dramatic but more likely to have a good result.

As Maeve was putting down the phone, Steve was not surprised to see that she had wound herself up into a state. She was pretty much talking aloud,

"I know why I'm so worried, it's not only that Marianne never does anything out of the ordinary, but I saw Susan this evening and she gave me that cryptic warning, what did she say? 'you need to know that it is not over. You must find the killer or the price you pay will be too high.' Was it to do with Marianne?"

Steve decided he had to tell her that Marianne wasn't the only one missing.

CHAPTER 26

ONE DOWN, ONE TO GO

Evening turned to night in Canterbury, they had walked themselves out, and Steve had exhausted his list,

"There is nothing more we can do tonight, but I don't want you to be on your own, so I suggest that I stay over, I can sleep on the sofa so that if anything happens I'll be here. Now, I suggest you have something to eat and try to rest, you will need your energy tomorrow."

Maeve went into the kitchen and nearly jumped as Edward spoke from behind her,

"Do we trust him, m'lady? Really trust him? He looks roguish to me, and a bit too familiar if you ask me. However, I am here, and I will stand watch tonight. Remember, I am good with fire and knives."

If she hadn't been so worried she would have laughed but it also made Maeve feel safe, she now had Steve, and Edward to keep an eye on Steve, and didn't have to go through this alone. She got some food, forcing herself to eat, thinking that she would need the energy. Her mind kept flipping between Susan's words, and knowing for certain that Marianne would never just take off without leaving a word.

She was so anxious she felt sick, so she called Ada and Orla, with a quick update. They put the phone on speaker-phone so that all three could talk, Ada said

"I had been wondering where the best place for us to be was too. I am worried about you, but then Marianne might come here...I'm glad that Steve is there with you, it can be tough on your own."

Maeve told them the news from Steve, that in Canterbury today another young man had been reported missing, and passed on Susan's cryptic comment.

Orla and Ada talked over each other,

"She definitely doesn't have a boyfriend at the moment" from Orla, and,

"Why didn't you say that before!", from Ada who went on, "if the spirits are talking to you, and they know something, you can demand information from them! Go, first thing in the morning and demand answers from them. My guess is that Susan doesn't have anything specific, but you could try her. Is there anyone else who has been holding out on you?"

Maeve's heart sank as she thought about Kevin, she knew that he had information. She filled the others in, Ada's experience came into play,

"Listen to me, you don't have to take shit from him, pardon my language, but really they do try it on sometimes, and actually you can and should take control. I know you are new at this and also in this case you really need the information, so maybe listen for a bit to get him on side then say 'enough from you' and demand some answers.That might work."

Ada didn't sound as confident as Maeve would have liked, but it was the best plan they had so far.

Earlier in Arras, as Marianne had been watching the family get ready, she was thinking to herself that she wasn't a fan of the sea. Beach holidays meant sand in everything, going blue from the cold, and being sticky from the salt water. It didn't matter if it was in Le Touquet or Margate, the results were the same. Nor did she want to spoil their fun. She could see Pascal on the phone preoccupied. She registered that she hadn't yet been seen by any of them yet, so it would be a good time to slip away unnoticed. Yet again she did something on the spur of the moment.

She made the decision that she would head home but slowly in her own time, she had really enjoyed today, just a little longer would be good. It was getting late. She had savings in her bank account, she could get a cheap room at the Ibis which was really central, and then take herself off for her favourite, a pizza at Le Vidoq!

Twice today she had that liberating feeling, it was good. Home by Sunday for sure but maybe by tomorrow evening would be enough of a break, she did love their Sunday morning rituals. She loved talking through her life with Maeve and Orla, they were a good team, they just hadn't been there for her recently. She really needed the time to herself to make sure she was prepared for the future, whatever it might hold. This trip was a good idea. Strange but good.

Maeve was still on edge, wringing her hands and constantly checking her phone. Steve, trying to find helpful anecdotes went on,

"..people can do strange things just before exams. I was at college with a guy doing theoretical physics, it was a no brainer, he was going to ace his finals. He didn't share with any of us what he was going through, but the stress got to him. And you won't believe what he did, it sounds like something from a movie but, he really did run away and join the French foreign legion.

"I saw him again, some years later, and heard the whole sad story, once he had signed up he realised the mistake he had made. Still, he wanted to see it through, putting himself in danger, feeling his life or death in the balance, to experience the real excitement of being alive. After this his exams were nothing. Then on his final training exercise he burst an eardrum so he never even got to see action.

"That's probably not the best example, what I mean is, rational people can do irrational things in moments of stress. But your Marianne is 18 years old, judging by you, she is likely to be well able to look after herself, and she probably needed a break. Having Ada over, and almost immediately the trauma of Anne, even if she missed the media mob. I could imagine wanting to get away from it all. Professionally speaking, you all get on well, don't you?"

Maeve nodded a vigorous 'yes'.

"So she is likely to come back in a day or so."

Appreciating the sympathy but knowing her daughter, Maeve came back with a quick

"But not Marianne! She is very thorough and precise about everything, she wouldn't do something like this without letting me know. It's not that she is not capable, but she would leave instructions. If not a phone message, then a note. This is really, really, not like her."

Meanwhile over in France, lying on her bed, happily tired Marianne was thinking, why was she really here? Was she running away from the fuss at home, or was she afraid of the exams? What was she expecting from her father, whom she loved but, who wasn't really a part of her everyday life.

She thought back to the times she had spent with Pascal, she could hear him saying, 'learn to love yourself for who you are'. He thought she pushed herself too hard, and would say, 'you are like your mother, always trying for more, bigger, better. This is not the way to happiness. You will be happy doing something you love. Do it as well as you can, and know that you are doing your best. Be that what it may, cutting hair, or being a doctor, it doesn't matter what it is, so long as you enjoy it. You don't have to be the best in the world, you have to know that you are doing the best you can, then you can be happy. Life is not a competition.'

In a moment of realisation she understood what he had been trying to say to her, and that he was right. She was afraid of failing, of letting people down, when she faced it, she realised that she was afraid of letting herself down. Again she could hear Pascal saying, 'I know you, you have done everything you can, haven't you? Now let go, and embrace the challenge, enjoy the challenge!'

Even if she hadn't seen him in person, Dad had managed to lift a weight from her, with that she fell sound asleep.

Of course, Maeve did not sleep well. Throughout the night, after what felt like a few minutes of sleep, she would wake with a guilty start, and would go over her relationship with Marianne, again, and again. Had she missed something, were there clues that she should have picked up on? Or worse. The thought that she didn't want to face, what if Marianne was the one lying in the grass?

By 5am she admitted to herself that there was no chance of sleep. Maeve had decided that there was enough light to see if she could find Kevin, and confront him. She slipped out of the house leaving Steve sound asleep on the sofa bed.

The morning air smelt fresh, of new growth, of an abundance of green and early blossom, the beauty of it all was jarring on Maeve. It was early enough that there were no cars around as she crossed the road up to the footpath through the woods, and on up the steep hill, and finally across the campus. Not knowing where exactly to find Kevin she headed over to Parkwood, the old launch site, walking the long way around to avoid the cordoned off area where she'd found Anne.

There he was, hands in his pocket, fag in his mouth, dirty shirt with grime from overuse around the shirt pocket where he kept his cigarettes,

"I knew you'd have to come back! Time for me now, do you? Well, I don't know that I want to tell you things now…"

. . .

For a moment Maeve thought that she had blown it, but no. There was never a chance that anyone would stop Kev from talking, from telling everyone how the world 'really' works.

"You see girlie, you're privileged, so you don't even look around you. You don't see who is really in charge. You may start off thinking I'm mad, but once you listen and check it out, you will see the truth.

"Of course there are the Jews. We all know that they have all the money, and don't you try and tell me that's not true. Just look at the banks, Rothschilds, and the Bank of England and the Fed in America are privately owned by?... you guessed it, the Jews… huh!

"But they aren't the only problem. The cabal who run the world, the Jews are in that, but there are others too. The Catholics! People don't look at the Catholics but they control one hell of a lot of the people.

"The word CABAL comes from the Secret Treaty of Dover where Charles II signed up to convert to Catholicism for money, bet you didn't know that. Look it up. You have to watch out for Muslims now too, they are the terrorists, it used to be the Irish with their bombs, now it's the Muslims. Got to keep them out."

Kevin hadn't drawn breath yet, and Maeve wondered how much of this rant she should listen to before asking or as Ada said 'demanding' information. Kevin felt her thoughts,

"Okay, okay I know you want some information but I have to give you the background or you won't see it either. And I need you to do something for me too."

He paused, drew breath and seemed to prepare himself to tell a long story.

"Canterbury is a big centre for members of the cabal to meet. The Canterbury Archeological Trust were finding things that people didn't want discovered.

"They won't admit it but they are close to finding 'anti gravity powder'. That would change the world. In theory it's buried under a huge stone, what's the biggest stone around here? You got it, the Cathedral. There are those of us who think it might be part of the Cathedral foundations. Why do you think 'they' are 'repairing' the stonework? It's a cover to poke about.

"Of course they work with those of us who know that the earth is flat. I have been up to the top of the Cathedral tower 236ft and you can see that the earth is flat. I mean the horsemen of the apocalypse come from the 'four corners of the earth' and if you look at the Canterbury cross you will see it's got the four points inside a circle, so it's a disk, Q.E.D. the earth is flat!"

Maeve was now shifting from foot to foot with impatience, as Kev continued,

"Anyway, you get where I'm coming from. So I had to work with the societies as a University staff member, I chose the rocket society to keep an eye on them and when I could, I would show them that they were being played by the elite, they were just the pawns in someone else's game.

"I met someone there who shared my views. We got on, but then it got a bit heavy. They were in with the Catholics, which was okay.....",

here, he seemed to hesitate so Maeve, trying to show that she had been following, chipped in,

"I thought you didn't like the Catholics." Back on track Kevin launched into,

"I don't but it doesn't mean that they don't know a thing or two about God!"

By this time Maeve had had enough; time to try Ada's strategy,

"Kevin, you seem to know a lot about what's going on around here. I demand that you tell me what you know about missing people."

She felt very strange saying it out loud but it seemed to have an effect on Kevin,

"What exactly do you want to know?"

He was a little cagey, almost sly, Maeve thought she would have to choose her words carefully,

"If someone is missing, where are they?"

Quick as a wink, Kevin replied

"I don't know, but if you asked me 'where are they kept?', I might have an answer."

Maeve was irritated, this wasn't the time to play word games,

"Sure, where are they kept?"

This time Kevin was very specific,

"In my opinion they are kept over there in St John Stone House."

He pointed over towards the main entrance to the University. There was a derelict building opposite the entrance. Maeve didn't trust him at all, but what else did she have to go on.

She tried one last time,

"Why do you think that?" Kevin didn't hesitate,

"Because the person who told me is a killer. They didn't give me proof, but the proof of the whole situation is there."

Maeve didn't want to spend any more time with Kevin than she absolutely had to, so with that she turned on her heel and left. As she retreated she could hear a fading Kevin shouting after her,

"Have a good look around and check the basement….there will be signs of the secret meetings too."

CHAPTER 27

THE SEARCH?

Maeve almost ran back to the house. Steve was already up and dressed,

"I thought you had walked out on me, before anything had even started!", there was fresh coffee on the table and a twinkle in his eye. Behind him Edward was fussing,

"It's all right m'lady I 'showed' him where things were, he didn't seem to notice, and he hasn't stolen anything yet. Better to have him be useful, if he's here at all." Edward finished with a sniff, nose clearly out of joint.

It washed right over Maeve who was in a hurry,

"Okay I have information."

Before she went on, Maeve mentally replayed what she had heard, thinking how much of it would make her sound as if she was losing her grip on reality. She would need to do an edit, select the key information, minimal description of Kevin but enough to convince Steve that this was serious.

She made breakfast as an excuse to take the time to martial her thoughts. When she had finished telling her story Steve was silent. They were sitting down over the breakfast table, on a second cup of coffee, surrounded by the remains of boiled egg and homemade brown bread toast.

Taking another mouthful of coffee, Steve started,

"You know, really, I have only just met you. What is it, a week ago that you came to the station?"

Maeve nodded thinking how much had happened in such a short space of time,

"Just under, it was a Sunday, last Sunday."

Steve went on,

"A week ago, I thought you might be a bit touched, a bit radio rental. But, I have a good nose for people and after I had spoken to you, I felt that you were telling me the truth, however hard it was for me to believe. Then you came in with the information on that hit'n'run, manslaughter, possible murder. How could you have known that? So you have been showing me more evidence that you are getting information from somewhere. Or, you are the one committing the crimes. Those are the only two explanations and I don't believe for a minute that you are a murderer. So, somehow you are getting information."

Maeve was listening intently, as her teaspoon was grinding against the bottom of her cup, which had already been well stirred. She had been going through her own internal ordeals, and simply hadn't thought how it might look from the outside. Of course Ada and Orla had made communicating with spirits seem normal.

"However," Steve resumed "the business with Anne, changed it again, this time you were getting information that might have stopped a crime if we had known how to use it."

Here he stopped, pouring out the dregs of the coffee pot, to give himself something to do as he reflected on the ramifications of what he had just said. In his world, this would be seen as crazy, as if he had lost the plot. Talking to ghosts was a 'no-no'. If he was going to act on any information that Maeve had received, then it would have to be down as an 'anonymous tip off'.

. . .

Maeve seemed to wake up from having been lulled into Steve's mindset.

"Wait a moment! This is my daughter we're talking about. I was thinking that you could gather a few strong policemen or women and that we could go and break the door down. I don't need to hear you decide whether I am telling the truth or not. I need help. Brute force. If you are not going to do that then I'll go myself. I have a crowbar somewhere."

She had jumped up and was already rummaging through tools under the stairs and pulled out the aforementioned crowbar with a triumphant 'gotcha'.

Steven had continued talking over her hasty actions with a

'

"You don't understand how the police work. This isn't my investigation. We haven't officially called Marianne in as a missing person yet. We are the only people who have come up with the concept that these deaths could be linked. We have no proof yet.

"So as far as the police are concerned, Marianne is a healthy young woman, not at risk. The other young lad is being followed up by my colleague, Tim Houghton who is a police inspector, and they will call in the local authority to organise a search, but that wouldn't start for at least 48 hours. Plus the young man might just have taken the weekend off, so everyone will wait till Monday."

What Steve hadn't explained, was the office politics that surrounded getting involved with other peoples cases, and that, in this unit, there was particular tension between Police Inspector Tim, and himself as a Detective Inspector. The chip on the shoulder that Tim had, because he hadn't been to university. Tim was a uniform policeman who had risen through the ranks. They were at the same level but Tim was going for promotion, and wanted to make sure that Steve didn't get there before him. In fact Tim was the one who had been behind a lot of the jeering or mocking of Steve.

He didn't say any of this because Maeve was already heading for the door, what he actually said was

"Stop!", as he caught her in the open door and held her by the shoulders physically stopping her from leaving,

"Wait a moment. It's dangerous. Plus, if you go over on your own, you'll be breaking the law, its private property and you will be treated like any thief 'breaking and entering'."

Maeve had lost all patience,

"So come with me and help!"

This was a total stand-off. Silence. Maeve's phone pinged, a text message. Steve let go of her as she reached down to look at her phone. It was from Marianne, *'Having a wonderful time. Didn't see Dad. Will be home this evening. Sorry I didn't call, batteries died, but you got my note. Love you. xxxxxx'.*

They had been standing with the front door open, a gust of wind caught the door and slammed it shut, the wind also disturbed Marianne's note which now floated down to the floor by their feet.

Relief flooded through Maeve,

"I knew she wouldn't do anything like this without leaving a message!" She had it in her hand,

"See, she didn't want to disturb me, that's why she left the note and didn't call. God knows how it ended up there...."

Steve stepped back, as she rambled on while putting the crowbar in the umbrella stand as if it was the most normal place to keep one. He recognised all the signs of shock and this time relief.

"I think a cup of tea is in order". By now, Steve knew the basics of the kitchen and thought it best he went to put the kettle on, what he didn't see was Edward hovering over his every move. Maeve was sitting on the bottom of the stairs feeling the worry dissolve as she collected herself.

Mugs in hand, they both went over the situation.

"Thank God, she's alive!", now Maeve could voice her worst nightmare. She had already texted Marianne to see what the plan was and should she come and pick her up? Equally she had messaged Pascal, Ada and Orla, the world could return to its proper place. When the happiness wave had begun to pass, Maeve said,

"So what about the message from Kevin? Could it relate to your young man, what's his name?"

Steve had to share more of the background politics than he really wanted to, but if he was ever to act on information that Maeve received, then they needed to work out how, and she needed to know that it would be at a distance. No running in with battering rams and Maeve leading the charge. But Steve had been convinced that Maeve really was communicating with spirits, who could help solve crime, and he promised that as a result he would take whatever actions he could. They officially shook hands on it. A deal.

As Steve left there were still a few lingering journalists hoping to get a picture of Ada and interviewing anyone they could catch coming or going from the house. But they were focused on Ray's house not Maeve's, so they didn't notice the policeman leaving.

Maeve got the vacuum cleaner out, put on Bruce Springsteen's upbeat 'Born in the USA' as loud as she dared and went on a cleaning blitz. By the time the house was back in order, Maeve was hot, sweaty and very happy. It had been interrupted by messages and calls. They had decided to meet up in Ada's for supper.

Orla had taken charge and had invited Pascal, Marie-Odile and the kids to come over too, encouraging them to take a cheap EuroTunnel day pass, saying it wasn't far and the kids could sleep in the car on the way back. So it had turned into a full scale surprise party for Marianne. Ada joining in with 'if it doesn't kill me, I must be cured!' Maeve was to pick Marianne up from Ashford train station and drive her over to Sandgate, theoretically to collect Orla and so keep the surprise.

It turned into one of those impromptu family gatherings that stays in the mind long after other 'important' events have dissolved from the collective memory. Life changes, life decisions, flowed through the conversation, there was time for everyone.

The weather was gorgeous, the afternoon turned to evening with never ending conversations, as they moved in and out of the house watching the children throwing stones on the beach, and the great food that Orla had 'assembled'.

As she said "..Assemblage is the new cooking" to which Maeve added,

"Which only works if you have delicious raw ingredients. Like the perfect brie, fresh bread, super thin prosciutto, at Ada's insistence and some really good red wine, from Pascal and Marie-Odile."

The atmosphere was warm and generous. Acceptance and support all round with the oft repeated 'no more secrets', relating as much to Marianne's secret getaway as to Ada's health, Orla's ambitions and of course Maeve's new 'friends'.

The addition of Pascal, Marie-Odile and the children, created the festive air, and the realisation that they needed to see each other more often. As much because they enjoyed each other's company, as because of the family connections.

The end of the evening had turned into a bit of a sing-song ranging from half remembers advertising jingles, to ballads, to Taylor Swift, as no one wanted it to come to a close. Finally it was Marie-Odile who looked at the time and suddenly everyone had to make their moves, with lots of hugs and kisses and 'see you soons'.

Ada and Orla had seen everyone off. They were coming back to Canterbury on Sunday, after Orla had cleaned up the house, which in fairness, she had offered to do. She really is becoming more mature, thought Maeve, as she and Marianne made their way through the countryside. At the same moment Marianne said it out loud.

"She is." Maeve was smiling at their similar thought processes, "And you have had the time to re-find yourself?"

Maeve said, more as a statement looking for confirmation than a question.

"Yes, I needed to come to that decision myself. I needed to know that there are other possibilities. And I needed to believe in myself, to know that I will not be defined by exams, I am more than that. Now with the pressure off I can study at my own pace. What will be, will be, but I know I will have done what I can."

Marianne sounded a little drowsy and fatigue eventually overcame her, she had begun to doze off, when Kamal spoke.

CHAPTER 28

THE PRESSURE IS ON

"Jesus Christ! You frightened the life out of me. You shouldn't creep up on people!' Maeve hissed startled, she almost, but didn't quite, wake Marianne.

Kamal, was calm,

"Is okay, she is asleep, and she can not hear me anyway. But you are distracted. I can feel that it is still urgent you find the killer. You need to do more research at the University." Maeve had wanted at least a little time to get her life back to some level of normality, but that clearly wasn't going to happen. She sighed as she asked,

"What am I looking for? I met Kevin, did you know him? I think he was like, Uni support staff, maybe he helped with equipment? Is he the guy I need to talk to?"

Kamal, thought before he spoke,

"Yes, I know who you mean. I love Britain but he is part of the English I do not like. He pretended to be a friend but he is racist. He doesn't always tell the truth, he twists facts. But he has information that will help you. Also you must look at others in the Uni. He was not alone."

Maeve was about to demand further names and details when she realised she was now talking to herself.

They had turned off the motorway just as Marianne woke, took a leisurely stretch and said

"I can see the Cathedral, almost home. It's only been two days but it feels like a real break."

Yes, Maeve thought, regardless of Kamal's comments there wasn't much she could do, it was late and tomorrow, a Sunday, normal offices are closed. She would do what she could but she might get a day to spend with the family. She needed to catch up with the mundane, like grocery shopping, then she could go full pelt on Monday morning.

Sunday turned out to be another one of those glorious, surprisingly hot, sunny days of early summer, it had now been officially declared a mini heat-wave. On the spur of the moment Maeve suggested,

"Why don't we carry on with the holiday feeling and do something touristy before Ada and Orla get here?"

Following Marianne's wishes they had had their Sunday morning croissants and coffee.

"We could pretend we really are tourists and do one of those walking tours? I had thought of being a guide so it could be market research?", said Marianne as she joined in the spirit of 'let's get out of the house so that we don't fall into a routine and miss the glorious day'.

For Marianne, today was the last day of her 'study break', so to enjoy it, spending time with Maeve, when it was just the two of them, was perfect. For Maeve, not being at home was an excellent idea. She hadn't seen any of the other neighbours since their gardens had been trampled by the TV crews, and that pushy journalist Simon had been harassing people to get any salacious gossip he could, to add to his 'good story'. She was expecting that she would have a lot of explaining to do about Ada, none of which she was ready to talk about.

Next door, Ruth and Ray had let them know that they were fine, and now wanted some time on their own to make plans. Maeve was keen to leave them in peace too.

Having checked online and booked their slot for a historic

walking tour of Canterbury, Maeve and Marianne headed off arm in arm glad to be on the move. As they made their way into town they were being silly, developing their 'tourist personae' and trying out adopted American accents.

They weren't rushing, and as they passed the Refectory coffee shop on St Dunstan's, Maeve noticed the unpleasant customer from Clothesline sitting at Maeve's favourite seat outside. With a start, Maeve now remembered who she was, and it clicked that she had also seen her in the cafe when she met Steve, but that's not how Maeve knew her.

While Maeve had still been working for the film festival, she had seen this 'Caroline', one of the funders, at a meeting where there was a massive row over money and the accounts. When she got home, Maeve had regaled the family with the story of 'cleavages at dawn', because, although they say women have no egos it is categorically not true. These women had gone at it with unnecessarily mean, acid comments, and absolutely no respect for each other. 'Caroline' was very well spoken, fastidiously dressed but clinically cold. She had absolutely no empathy for the local team working on a shoestring. At the time Maeve had just finished reading 'The Psychopathy Test', and thought she fit the category as a confirmed psychopath. Luckily, Caroline was sufficiently self important that she hadn't paid attention to any of the other staff, so wouldn't have noticed Maeve. Hence Maeve was able to walk confidently on by, looking straight ahead. One mystery solved, she thought to herself, imagining that this was another step in life returning to normal. She was wrong.

Arriving at the Buttermarket just in time to join their booked eleven o'clock walking tour, they were still a bit giddy and definitely the naughty ones at the back. As they walked the tour got more interesting, their guide really knew his stuff. In fact when they had stopped laughing at each other, and took a good look he was handsome, tanned, clean shaven and sharply dressed, he didn't look like the usual fare. Well spoken and knowledgeable he'd shown them the Roman bathhouse under the old Waterstone's shop; Elizabeth I's ceiling in Cafe

Nero; the pilgrim's hostel; Dickens' part of Canterbury; and the largest, possibly oldest theatre in England, now the Three Tuns pub, which sits on part of the stage of the Roman theatre. One of the group put forward the theory,

"If only the ghosts could talk, I bet there would be some hairy tales!", to which he replied,

"That would be on the other kind of tour, there is a 'ghost hunters tour' if you are interested."

Their guide seemed a little dismissive, but Maeve and Marianne were both very happy to avoid the ghost hunters tour, they had had enough contact with the spirit world for the moment.

As this was the end of the walk, and as they were standing outside the Three Tuns, they offered their guide a drink in the pub, which he accepted. Most of the group drifted away, a few lingered with specific questions,

"Is it true that there are tunnels under Canterbury to sneak in and out of the Cathedral?"

And those showing off that they had done their background research,

"Was St Martin's a Mithraic temple before it was a Christian Church?"

All of which he answered with patience,

"Yes there are tunnels under the city as you would expect given its age and the rock formation. Yes we believe that St Martin's Church was a temple dedicated to the Roman cult of Mithras. Thank you for all the interesting questions, I hope you enjoy the rest of your stay in Canterbury."

Which was a reasonably elegant brush off, and arrived in time for the cool lagers that Maeve and Marianne brought to their table.

He began with

"Thank you. You both arrived a little after the others, I'm Tony Blackstone, and you are?" They introduced themselves and explained that they were in fact locals. Tony said,

"I thought you might be. I am a sort of local having been here for the last ten years."

Maeve was still intrigued,

"Are there really tunnels? I read about one being opened up in the Cathedral, but really it was just a passage under the main stairs to the altar. And if you don't mind my asking how do you know so much? Are you part of the Archeological Trust?"

He smiled

"First things first. Yes it is believed that there is a tunnel from Buttermarket to the Cathedral, I guess for monks who missed the curfew, and yes some of this is my field, I am a lecturer in Archeology, at the University of Kent.

"I like all of modern history, I think of it as a soap opera, the connections with Charles Dickens and Rupert Bear are fun, like gossip. But my real area is early medieval, so I spend quite a bit of time in the Cathedral. They have an extraordinary library. Kent County Council also has a lot of fascinating documents, if you are interested",

He seemed to sense they might be losing interest. In fact, far from getting bored, Maeve had been wondering if he could help with some context around Kevin,

"Maybe you could help?, I have been doing some research into UKC",

she said while looking at Marianne to make sure that she would go along with her cover story,

"we're looking at Universities for my younger daughter and she asked about extra curricular activities? Would it be okay to meet up sometime for a coffee and a chat, so that you can tell her what it's really like?"

Maeve knew it was a bit cheeky but he was cute, and Orla was a better liar than Marianne. Tony, a gregarious person by nature, looked flattered that Maeve so clearly found him attractive. He also gave a sense that he might be aware that he was 'God's gift' to women, smiled a confident,

"Sure, anytime."

Then a pause as he considered what he had just said and came back with,

"Actually, I guess you are going to take me up on that, so

what I really mean is, anytime I'm not in class or underground. I have to finish up some work I'm in the middle of right now, and the documents are held here in town in the Cathedral archives but if you are serious, then can I suggest that later today would work? Up at the University. I know I will be tied up during the week and Sunday's are the best day for me."

They laughed as they walked home picking up a few bits for supper as neither had the energy to face a full on supermarket shop. Marianne was doing the post-mortem,

"Yes, he was definitely good looking, and interesting, but did you not smell the aftershave? I would call that overpowering! So regardless of his age, not my type, plus he might be a little young for you Mum? Frankly, for you, I prefer your policeman. He may be a conservative with a small 'c', but he means well, has a nice smile, and cheeky twinkly eyes which say he might be fun if we didn't only meet him when there was a crisis."

Marianne was thinking as she spoke and went on,

"Upon mature reflection, that is a good sign. He is good in a crisis, and we know that for sure!"

Maeve laughed indulgently, enjoying the more adult relationship she was developing with Marianne. She was feeling pretty good about things in general. Yes, she did have work to do but now she might have an ally, who was good to look at, and well he had almost made it a date. Her energy and good humour had been restored by last night's deep sleep along with the embracing family time. Life was certainly interesting and she was ready to face it.

It was mid afternoon when Steve called,

"We have had a situation change at this end. The missing bloke, Adam Goodman is his name, he's not a teacher. He was due to give a lesson but actually he's a PhD student at the University.

"More importantly his family have now been in touch,

and what we didn't know is that he is a Type 1 diabetic. The family say that he always takes some emergency insulin with him, and some sugar snacks, you know those fruit bars, and some glucose sweets. All of which means he's okay for a day or two but he is likely to suffer hyperglycemia after that. So may be in a daze or fall into a coma. Everyone is different so no one knows exactly how long he can survive without insulin. He might be okay, but it's a matter of days maximum."

"What is he studying?", was Maeve's first question.

"Archeology. I don't have access to all of the files and as I explained, I am acting in a supporting role here, helping out a colleague… any information that you can find out from your side might speed things up and might be the very thing that saves his life!"

As Steve said the word 'Archeology', Maeve ever the optimist thought 'is this just weird or is the universe trying to send me some help?' The question she might have asked was, 'or is the universe leading me astray?'

CHAPTER 29

A STEP TOO FAR

Adam was now the most urgent focus of Maeve's attention, she knew a bit about diabetes, enough to be aware that if they don't get their insulin in time people die of it. It's not an exaggeration. Time was of the essence. This didn't just focus her attention, it put a lot of pressure on her, this was both the test that she could do some real good in the real world, and how she could turn her burden into a gift.

As soon as she put the phone down from Steve, she talked to Marianne, giving Marianne the job of the family logistics for the rest of the day with a promise that she, Maeve, would devote her time to supporting Marianne starting tomorrow morning. Marianne, laughed at her mother,

"You always do this, you need something to drive you. It's fine. I get it. This time, it really is urgent, and someone's life is counting on you. But even if it wasn't, you would make whatever you were doing important. That's all good and I love you for it. But I am not counting on you to give things up for me. However, I am asking you to save enough time for us too."

Maeve was duly chastised, recognising herself in Marianne's description, she gave her daughter a hug and a kiss,

"I am so glad you are my daughter. You are wonderful, and yes I promise we will still have family time."

Steve had told Maeve that the police team were working with the local authority to set up a search party. First the police community unit would start with a small team checking out the places that Adam was known to visit. If they found anything, he would let her know immediately. If they didn't, it would widen, and the local authority was already contacting volunteer groups, to have them on standby for a campus wide search before it was too dark.

The University seemed to be a linking factor, but Maeve was a little disappointed that there was no connection to the rocket society, as that seemed to link Susan, to Kamal, and Kevin.

She had been planning to do some online research into their members and activities to see what that threw up. Now she thought, if I can do some Googling before I meet him at least I can check that out with Tony. If he doesn't have the answers offhand, he will be able to access any information we might need, because he's a member of staff.

Kamal's warning made sure that she wanted some additional info to cross reference Kevin. But, should she trust this man that she had only just met, with her newly acquired secret powers? She absolutely needed the information, just how much should she tell him? He had been very dismissive of the 'ghost hunters tour', would this make him think she was deranged? She thought she would have to take the risk, they were running out of time. They had agreed to meet for a coffee at 4.30pm in the Gulbenkian cafe on campus.

By this time Ada and Orla had arrived, and Marianne had them up to speed. Orla said,

"As you have already brought me into this, I am coming with you, plus I think I need to check this guy out too."

Ada hadn't wanted to be too pushy so she had waited a moment before suggesting,

"Why don't you get Orla and Marianne to do the internet research, and you go and see if you can get anything out of Susan? Then maybe pop up to the campus, and if you have time you could talk to Kevin too? I can make the tea."

They all looked at her, this was a new, more humble Ada. The media fiasco had clearly had an impact. It was an excellent plan, everyone set to.

Maeve was walking as fast as she could. Susan was already waiting for her in the park,

"I knew you needed to ask me something, and yes you are right it's really urgent."

Maeve went through a number of questions and Susan was thoughtful as she answered,

"Yes I knew Kamal, he was a funny guy. Why the rocket society? Sometimes the foreign students would get involved with activities to have something to do, as a way to meet people. But Kamal was passionate about rockets, good to do fun experiments with, but otherwise he seemed to avoid contact with students particularly the other Iraqis."

Maeve was under time pressure so prompted her "Kevin?"

"Yes. Vaguely. I can see him, always smoking cigarettes. He didn't smell good, so I didn't go too near him. Anyway, he didn't like foreigners. He talked a lot, I overheard him talking to the others, 'we needed to destroy the elite'. He didn't like women, or gay men. But he knew everything about the university. He will have useful information for you."

Maeve was impatient, this added colour but wasn't tangible information. She hoped the girls were having better luck. Orla met her on her way back to the house, saying

"I'll brief you on the way. Let's take the car, that hill is a killer when you're in a rush."

Maeve smiled, Orla was being very practical, good to have on the team.

On their way, Orla told her what they had found. Adam had come to UKC last autumn to start his PhD, his subject was early medieval archeology, and the great reveal was that his PI was one Dr. Tony Blackstone.

"PI is principal investigator which means that they applied for the grant that pays for the work, it doesn't mean that they actually do any of the work. They might, but they don't have to."

"Do we know the subject of his PhD?", Maeve asked. She had remembered Tony saying sometimes he had no signal, so it sounded like something underground or in a remote area away from any signal.

"No, well, I couldn't find anything, it seems that they don't say until it's finished and published. But, my guess is that it will have something to do with the Cathedral. I mean why else would you come to Canterbury?"

Orla was an efficient researcher and had a good command of the facts. Maeve knew they didn't have much time,

"So what do we say to Tony? Tell him the truth or go on with our ruse that you are trying to find the right University and I want to keep you close to home?"

They were parking the car as Orla said,

"Go with the story, we might put him off with talking ghosts. Your line is 'my daughter has been telling me tales of mysterious deaths connected to the University' do you know anything to set her at ease? That way we can ask some direct questions."

"Good plan." Maeve was enjoying seeing Orla in this new light.

They were both very aware that time was ticking by. Maeve definitely wasn't in the right frame of mind to check out a potential new man. It was a good thing that Orla was there. It turned out that she had bumped into Tony before, when she was doing her admissions story, so this worked out fine. She was great at wildly exaggerating lurid tales, to lead Tony into revealing what he knew.

"Yes, I knew Kevin, poor man. Helpful with practicalities of University life, heating, lighting and such like. Of course he was a conspiracy theorist, sometimes I worried that he might have acted on his theories. He probably knew where all the bodies are buried so to speak,"

Tony laughed at his own joke,

"but there's nothing suspicious about his death, sad but not of concern, he broke his neck falling down some stairs in his own home. Nothing to worry about. And if Orla does decide to study here I can always keep an eye on her."

Tony smiled a little patronisingly.

"Now if you will excuse me, something urgent has come up. One of my students has gone AWOL, probably just lost his keys, the family are making a fuss so I have to go. But always happy to share my experience, when I have the time. So don't hesitate to book in another chat."

He flashed a smile at Maeve, and left them to finish their drinks. As soon as he had gone Orla didn't hold back,

"Mum, don't you even look twice at him, he is so full of himself he would be unbearable. He is too neat, too clean, and in case didn't you notice he has one ear pierced, so either he is too trendy for his age, or he might not be interested in women."

This made Maeve laugh,

"So glad I asked your opinion. Just because he is not your type, which I guess might be more earnest, doesn't mean he wouldn't do for me."

It was time to check in with Steve, he gave his update first, so far they had no trace of Adam. He had left his rooms as normal, and from the stock left in the fridge, they had been able to work out how much insulin he had with him. It was getting critical. The search had been escalated, they were working out the routes across the campus right now.

With her fingers crossed and wishing that she had more hard facts, Maeve said,

"I am convinced that there is a serial killer. If there is and Adam is being held, then I believe that it's in the derelict building St John's Stone House."

Steve replied with the unhelpful

"You had better be right."

Maeve thought that Tony may be full of himself but at

least he was entertaining. He had lots of stories about his adventures, and wasn't putting her under any pressure. Right now, that made him pretty attractive.

Steve also crossed his fingers when he pushed the team to divert men to the derelict site. His nemesis Tim had come in with a,

"No one goes in there, not since the fire, unless they are up to no good, or are hiding out. Is that what you're saying Steve? On a hunch you want to divert precious resources to go on a wild goose chase, your own pet project? This really isn't the time for that."

Having made his statement, Tim hadn't tried to stop them. In fact Tim was quietly hoping they would go and it would be a waste of time and he could heap scorn on Steve. Egos meant that they could never have a proper joint planning session. Tim had been keeping Steve on the sidelines. Normally Steve would just step back, but this time there was a life at stake. Weighing on his mind was the fact that if he had acted earlier on Maeve's tip off he might have been able to save Anne.

Maeve was desperate to know what was happening. She didn't know how she could get involved. She didn't have to wait long.

~

I have been getting more strung out, I can feel the next release close. Cat and mouse. Yes stretching the moment definitely increased the potential pleasure. In a mundane way it's like smelling the coffee but not drinking it. You can hold this moment too long and destroy the enjoyment. The trick is to get the timing right. Hold or move?

. . .

I know they are looking. Do I have the nerve to hold? The pleasure will be intense.

CHAPTER 30
DISASTER

Police descended on St John's Stone House, with blue lights flashing and the battering ram or the enforcer, the 'big red key' as they liked to say. They probably didn't need it, but as time was of the essence this was likely to be the quickest way of getting in.

No one really believed that Adam was being held, the general view was that he might have gone to have a butcher's and got stuck inside. That was reasonable. There was that embarrassing incident that went viral earlier in the year when a policeman on another force got stuck in the toilet and his colleagues had used a battering ram to get him out. At least this time it was a member of the public. And it was urgent.

They smashed their way in. Heaps of debris were blocking the doorway. The reason the building was derelict was abundantly clear. The fire had almost completely destroyed the first floor, most of which had collapsed onto the ground floor. They could smell stale urine and cold ash. Once fully inside they could see the rat tracks, and nests made by the occasional rough sleeper along with discarded plastic milk bottles still with traces of congealed sour milk and the telltale marks of drug use.

But, no one had been inside this building in months, if not years. Tim set to ridiculing Steve immediately. Many of the rank and file thought it had been a reasonable call, but they weren't going to side with a detective over one of their own uniform coppers. Steve had known this was a risk, but it was a risk worth taking if it saved a life. Now his name was mud, and Tim would make sure that everyone knew it. Frustrated and angry, Steve said nothing at all.

Given the critical situation for the missing Adam, they didn't have time to dwell on it now. Steve knew the mocking would be relentless over the next weeks and months, but right now they needed to get back on track. Clearly talking to the dead was not going to help. Let's refocus on traditional policing methods, he thought.

Get the volunteer search underway. Tim would get one team on the campus first. Thinking wider he reflected that they probably needed to start looking at the rivers, this was more for a body than a living person, but as each moment passed, that became increasingly more likely to be the outcome. Before he could get on with the real police business, Steve had to speak to Maeve.

Steve hadn't been able to vent his frustration to his colleagues, so Maeve got it all, both barrels. Steve didn't mean to be cruel, but he was.

"I don't know what you thought you were doing, but no one in their right mind would provide false leads without having the express intention of wasting police time. Is that what you wanted?

"Right now it's critical that we find this young man as soon as humanly possible and you have cost us valuable hours that we just don't have. Keep your amateur sleuthing to yourself and leave this to the professionals."

Maeve was completely crushed.

Up to that very moment, Maeve had been on such a high. She had had a strong sense of purpose, she knew how she could save the world, this bit had been the test. Now in one short phone call, it all came crashing down.

. . .

Ada had heard Maeve's side of the call, followed by the silence and then the sobbing; which she guessed were tears of anger, and frustration combined with a dose of self pity. Coming into the sitting room with two mugs of hot tea, Ada shut the door behind her so that they wouldn't be disturbed.

First Ada handed Maeve the box of mansize tissues, with a,

"Do they think women have less tears?" which brought the drift of a smile across Maeve's face as she pulled out a tissue, blew her nose, and wiped her eyes. Then Ada handed her the tea without saying anything. Maeve caught her breath, and the hiccuping subsided, all the while Ada was sipping her tea watching her. Ada spoke first,

"Life's a funny old thing. You think you understand everything, you know what to do, and then something happens that turns everything on its head."

Pause. Maeve wasn't really paying attention. Ada resumed.

"You know that's not how it works. In fact, life throws things at you, to see how you react. It's what you do next that counts."

Maeve was listening, but stayed silent, looking at Ada.

"Well, it's only a week since I nearly died. That's a shocker I can tell you. I realised that I wasn't ready to die, I still had things to fix. While I was in the hospital I made the decision that if I lived, the first thing I had to do was to tell you the truth, I owed you an explanation."

Ada stopped to take a sip of her tea, Maeve said nothing.

"Well, it's onc thing to make a promise to yourself. It's a lot harder to do it. I promised myself I would tell you everything. I know this sounds like I'm rambling again, but I will get to the point, this story is about 'what you do next'."

"This is extremely hard for me. I will only tell you this once, never to be mentioned again. I don't even know if I will be able to manage it but this is the right time. If I don't tell you now, I will have time to start making up reasons to stay quiet just as I have done in the past. Here goes."

Maeve had been completely flattened after the phone call, she had no strength left to say anything, so she sat back, both hands wrapped around her mug, grateful for the comfort of the hot drink. Ada went on,

"Many years ago back in Ireland, I wasn't long married, when joy of joys I found out I was pregnant. My God, I was so ignorant. I knew nothing about having a baby. I was convinced everything was going to be wonderful. The priest was delighted for us. The doctors were on hand. Sure, what did I have to worry about? I got through morning sickness, tough, but fine. The middle trimester was great, I was full of beans, enjoying feeling the baby kick and the bump grow."

Ada paused, gathering the courage to tell this story that she had buried for over forty years, and not knowing quite how to get the words out.

"At the time we lived in Co. Louth and our local hospital was Our Lady of Lourdes. It was 1979, and rural Ireland was a different place then. The Catholic Church had great power over our lives.

"I didn't know it but there were many against the procedure of the Caesarean section. Although Caesareans were common in many hospitals there were those doctors with strong Catholic convictions who wanted something more 'natural', something they thought would help women get pregnant again and have large families. Well, as I am sure you have guessed by now, you were a big baby."

She stopped again, this time when Maeve turned to look at Ada she could see the tears flowing down her cheeks. No sobbing, just tears, and Ada was looking straight ahead as she said,

"If I look at you now, I won't be able to finish the story, so look away, please. I need to say this once and that will be that."

Ada started again,

"There is a word for it now, it's called symphysiotomy. For Christ's sake, I trusted these people and they did this to me."

Ada was struggling with the anger she felt while trying to get the words out so that Maeve would know what had actually happened,

"I was in labour, in the hospital and they explained that due to the size of the baby they were going to carry out a procedure. They didn't ask permission, they didn't explain what it was. Your father wasn't there, men often weren't. Then they showed me the saw. I said no, there must be a mistake, that couldn't be for me. They told me to be quiet and said I had no choice, I shouted for help but no one came. They held me down and with a local anaesthetic they sawed the pelvis, through the bone."

Ada paused for a breath,

"Thank God, that saw didn't touch you. Later I found out that others weren't so lucky, about one in ten of the babies suffered. After that I don't remember much, it was over very quickly and there you were, wonderful, perfect, wrapped up and handed to me. You were the prize."

Ada stopped and wrapped her arms around herself.

"Then after that horror, I was treated like all the other new mothers. Get up and walk, they said. The sooner you get back to normal the better. It was as if they didn't want to recognise what they had just done. I had a broken pelvis but they wanted to pretend that I had a normal birth. This was cruel, sadistic. The pain. I don't think that there are words to describe it. And all alone. Get back to normal, they said."

At this Ada was rocking herself back and forth, the tears continuing to flow. Maeve couldn't bear it, she filled her hands with tissues and wrapped her arms around Ada, love, tears and pain all merged.

Ada accepted the embrace but wouldn't look at Maeve, determined to finish she went on,

"I promised myself that I would never speak of it again. Also that I would never have another child. Your father didn't fully understand what had happened. He still dreamed of his precious son. Well, time is a healer, I recovered, but as you know I am not the most athletic."

Ada gave a short laugh,

"Yes, 'not athletic' is what I used to say, or my 'hip' problems. In reality I learned to live with the pain, I haven't had a day pain free since then.

'We moved to England. And to Middlesex, that was for the hospital, your father thought 'something could be done'. I was prepared to talk to the doctors because I was looking for pain relief. But I was never, ever, going through another birth, when he realised that, we grew apart.

"Of course he blamed you for his lost son. It became a habit to blame you for everything. His resentment made him mean to you. When I tried to help, to protect you, that made it worse. So I had to pretend I didn't care. My escape was my gift to be able to talk to the dead. That was my way to prove that they couldn't take my life away from me. Sadly, you also had to pay a high price, and I could say nothing. By the time I could, the words wouldn't come. I had clenched my teeth for so long they just wouldn't open. I tried a few times but nothing happened."

This time Ada turned to Maeve before going on,

"I am so, so sorry, for your lost childhood. You were the only thing that made life worth living."

This time the hugs were two sided, they had really found each other.

"This heart attack made me realise, that you have to know, I can't let this destroy your life too. And just now, I heard what happened. You have a gift and you are strong. You can recover from anything. Don't let your sense of self get in the way. If I had spoken out I could have done something to help others. You are stronger than me."

Ada stopped talking and they just hugged each other in silence. Maeve couldn't find any words to say. She was so shocked, so horrified and at the same time felt so guilty, anything she might say would be wrong. She just wanted to hold on to Ada because that was all she could do to make things a little better.

It was Marianne who came in first. She had prepared a pasta bake with fresh basil, mozzarella and tomato sauce. Marianne and Orla had seen the closed door, caught the tone of the conversation and kept out until there was silence. Knowing that Ada and Maeve would talk to them when they were ready, the two girls came in with steaming bowls of food. Marianne said,

"I know you need time, but this guy Adam doesn't have time. So Orla and I need to eat before joining the search party on the campus. We think you should eat too, even though we know you aren't coming out with us, you still need to eat!"

It was the break Ada and Maeve needed, to give them both time to recover some sort of equilibrium before saying anything meaningful. Ada smiled as she looked at Maeve and said,

"Haven't you got two wonderful daughters! And don't I have one too."

Now the girls knew they had been right to keep out of it, they had never seen such emotion pass between their mother and grandmother. As they ate Marianne explained that the school had been in touch looking for volunteers in the area, so long as they had parental approval. The aim was to create a campus wide line to walk through the grounds in case he had collapsed, was in a coma, and just not visible. As Marianne finished talking, Orla took the plates into the kitchen, loaded the dishwasher, grabbed their jackets and was standing by the door shouting

"Hurry up! Let's go."

There were times when they were glad to have each other as sisters.

With that they left Maeve and Ada still sitting much where they had been when they came in with the food. Maeve made herself and Ada some fresh tea and said,

"I feel like my stomach has been hollowed out. What a shit daughter I have been. I never even tried to see things from your side. Never tried to guess that things might not actually be the way they seemed on the surface."

Ada replied,

"You were trying to get your father's approval. He pushed me out, and you had to do that too, just to manage each day. You don't need to say anything now. God willing, we will have time. We both have a lot to process. Maybe I will learn to talk. It's all in the past now. We are here, we are alive, today. That's what matters. "

It had been so emotionally draining that Ada needed to change the subject,

"Now about your gift and what about this young lad? Did one of the spirits lead you astray? They can be bastards! As I said, it's not about what happened, it's all about what you do now."

Maeve, realising that her own drama had really just been a dint to her sense of self, gave a sigh.

"You're right, I thought I had this thing sorted. I thought I could really help. But I can't."

She paused for a moment,

"After listening to what happened to you, I can see that my pride was hurt but that's about it. And of course, it turns out that I am not some superhero dashing to the rescue. I have just been made a fool of by some unpleasant spirit.

"Yes, Kevin, I think he was on his own crusade. He had fallen for this conspiracy theory and he wanted to show that he was right. I didn't trust him, but there was nothing else to go on."

With that Maeve put her head in her hands,

"Mum, I don't know if I can do this. Now I know for sure that whatever you say, I am not as strong as you. All those unhappy spirits looking for closure. What if this happens again? If I get it wrong again, I don't think I can keep going."

Ada was indignant on behalf of Maeve,

"Don't be ridiculous of course you are! Sure aren't you the one that always stood up for your friends at school? Ms Champion of Justice, coming home to ask what a trade union was and could you form one. It's one of the wonderful things about you Maeve, you will always go into battle for the underdog. Now let's pull ourselves together and see what we can do."

Ada breathed in, straightened herself and said

"Take a ten minute break in the garden, breathe some fresh air, then come back and we will make a plan together."

Maeve was glad to be told what to do right now.

And Ada, she felt a lot lighter, a weight had been lifted. She had one more key piece of information to give Maeve, and she didn't think they had the time to leave it for another day.

CHAPTER 31

DANGER

Maeve stood outside in her garden breathing in the early evening air, the trees with new green were tall above the incline of the back garden, the scent rising from the earth, the drift of sweet blossom. It was grounding Maeve. She couldn't process all of Ada's story, she knew it would take time. Now she needed to breathe to centre herself. Maeve was deep in her mindfulness exercises, when she was disturbed by a,

"Hello there neighbour!"

This was the way Anne used to shout over the fence when she had some veg to share, briefly Maeve thought it was a voice in her own head. She looked over towards the fence and sure enough, there was Anne. Anne went straight on with,

"I don't want to bother you but there are a few things I need and some you need."

This was the last straw, it overwhelmed Maeve, she said,

"I'm sorry Anne, I can't. I can't deal with this right now."

Maeve turned and went straight back into the house.

"Ada it doesn't matter how much you say I can, I can't. I am not ready for this. It's all too much."

and with that, Maeve retreated to her bedroom and slammed the door shut. Part of her knew she was being pathetic, adolescent, but she needed to slam something and she needed to be alone. No one else could fix this. How could she make it stop. It was all engulfing, overpowering, her emotional roller coaster had taken her up to the highest point and come crashing down, and then down again, with no relief. Ada's story meant she had to rethink her childhood. She had to let go of the resentment which had been a driver for her actions and now she had to handle new feelings of guilt.

Maeve also had to face up to her 'gift'. The people who talked to her in the hospital, maybe she could handle that, mostly they just wanted to say goodbye. But the ones like Susan, Kamal and Kevin were serious, these were murders and they needed a real champion, someone who would fight for them. Thinking of Kevin, Maeve added, and it has to be someone who can be tough and handle them too! What was that old quote, 'Life does not put things in front of you that you are unable to handle', Maeve used to think that was true, right now, she was not at all sure. She needed to clear her head and decide who she was and who she wanted to be, hero? Mother? Daughter? Or all three?

So they are looking the wrong way. I can play a little longer. Maybe I can send them on another wild goose chase. Maybe I won't. Exciting.

Up on the University campus things were getting underway. They had pulled in anyone who knew Adam, friends, lecturers, support staff, dividing them up so that they could be shared out amongst the volunteers. The police community safety officers were organising the volunteers into logical groups to sweep across designated areas of the campus, making sure that altogether they would cover the entire open ground.

Marianne and Orla had joined the search, and just in

time Orla spotted Tony Blackstone, she quickly pulled Marianne into another group hissing

"Let's avoid him if we can."

They were told what to do. Their group was to form at the back of Woody's bar, just beyond the turning circle facing the green 'open' space, which was actually under cover of trees. They were to form a line with about a metre between each person and walk as one.

As they gathered Orla heard a voice behind her,

"You're her daughter, aren't you? They say it runs in families. Anyway I don't have time, you need to know things. He has access to underground rooms in the Cathedral. We were looking for the anti-gravity powder and he could take us into locked rooms, he has keys, because of the archives."

Orla turned to see an overweight scruffy man with greasy hair in maintenance overalls,

"Are you Kevin?" she was sharp and to the point with her question.

"Yes",

Kevin was a little reluctant, but trying to win her over he went on.

"I know, I know, it wasn't wrong, I just wanted to know if the cabal were there, they are behind it all, everything, and she made them look, anyway they hid it, they hid the information it would never've been in plain sight. Bloody coppers didn't look properly!"

He smiled, very pleased with himself that his plan had worked even though he was disappointed with the result,

"But this time he will kill again, it's what you want to find not what I want, this is where you will find him."

Orla was shoo-ing him away,

"I don't believe a word you say, what do you mean rooms under the Cathedral? Archives, access to locked places, anti-gravity powder? Do you think I would believe you when you have proved yourself to be a liar!"

Marianne was looking at her strangely,

"Are you talking to yourself?"

This made Orla laugh,

"It's just the way it is, but he is not a good spirit so I won't talk to him. And now, 'poof', I can't even see him anymore, that door is closed."

Marianne was a little concerned,

"Sure you are okay?"

Orla could be overconfident but there was conviction in her voice,

"Never better!"

They were still milling around, and getting into the starting position when Orla heard a

"Psst, over here."

Looking under the branches she realised that she was looking towards Parkwood Rd, and there under the trees was Anne beckoning her over.

"I don't want to bother your mother, she is having a difficult moment, but there isn't much time, so can you give her a message?"

Orla walked right over to Anne so that no one would overhear the conversation and asked,

"How are you?"

Anne smiled,

"You are a good girl, always were. I'm fine. In fact, I'm happy here, I'd appreciate it if you would pass that on, to Ray and the children. But the urgent business, is that I know who killed me. On this side, it was a bit like waking up from a fuzzy sleep, my head is clear now. And once the family are okay and I have said goodbye, I am happy to stay here. But urgently, I need your mother to tell people the truth, and to stop him otherwise I will be tied here in Parkwood. Tell her this….."

Orla, dashed over to Marianne,

"I have to do something in town. When this walk is over, go and tell Mum and Ada that Anne remembers. I need to check it out but if she's right, we'll find the guy Adam. I am pretty sure that he is not here but finish this first because after Kevin, we don't know who to trust and Anne's dementia might be fooling her."

Marianne was of the view that they needed to do the logical as well as the spiritual, so she agreed and gave Orla a sisterly warning,

"Don't take any risks."

Orla grinned

"Moi? Take a risk? Certainly not an unnecessary one!" with that she was gone.

They had finished their walk through in about half an hour. Nothing. The other teams were still going but Marianne's lot were told that they were done for today. The days had been lengthening but it was now definitely dusk.

Marianne was hoping that she had done the right thing by staying with the search and that Orla would already have got home before she did. It's good to hope, but sometimes that can get you, or someone else, into serious trouble.

I could feel the excitement rising. The possibility of two at the same time was being offered to me on a plate, that was delicious enough to hold out for. And right under their noses too. I am so clever. I am the cat with two mice. And it's almost supper time.

CHAPTER 32
THE CHASE

Maeve had been walking in small circles in her bedroom, wishing she had more time, more space, and no pressure. Ada's revelation had stunned her and she just didn't know what to do. She wanted the whole world to stop dumping on her and give her some space.

As she thought that, she noticed that aphorism that she had remembered, which someone had sent on a card, propped on the window 'life doesn't put anything in front of you that you are unable to handle.' Really? She sighed. As she looked around the room she started noticing the other ones that she had gathered over time.

'What you choose also chooses you.' - Kamand Kojouri; 'Today is the first day of the rest of my life' - Charles Dederich; landing on the last one 'Always ask yourself: What will happen if I say nothing?' - Kamand Kojouri. For the first time they seemed to be talking directly to her, actually pretty much shouting at her. As if the world had been trying to tell her something that she had set herself against, and refused to see. She had kept these particular cards, as they registered with her, it felt like she had been keeping them for today.

In fact it was her decision to deal with her relationship with Ada, which had started this whole adventure. She knew it would take time, time would heal her relationship with Ada, today's story was momentous, but now Maeve understood at a profound level, that there was real love on both sides. Both of them needed to reset the past, but luckily, they were in a stage of their lives where they could take however long it needed to do that.

Maeve's mind moved on, she also knew she couldn't live with herself if she didn't try to help save this young man's life. This was another tremendous shift in the very sense of who she was.

She decided that she had to embrace her gift, to set it at the feet of the problem. She would not forgive herself if she could have helped and didn't. Once Maeve made that decision she knew she could regain control of her life. Now she could talk to Ada, in the certain knowledge, that Ada would help.

When Marianne arrived home, Maeve and Ada were surrounded by paper with random notes, maps and sketches. Maeve could immediately see that Marianne didn't have any positive news.

"Where's Orla?", she asked as Marianne was already starting to explain,

"Orla spoke to Kevin, I could only hear her side of the conversation and it was about access to archives in the Cathedral grounds, some underground room, and she said something about anti-gravity powder?

"Then she walked over towards Parkwood Rd, seemed to be talking to someone, she dashed back in a hurry and told me to tell you both that 'Anne remembers' and then that she had to check something out in town which if Anne was right, could lead to wherever Adam is. I guess she went into the Cathedral….?"

Marianne left the question hanging.

"Shit, shit, double shit" burst out Maeve, "Anne tried to talk to me about an hour ago, she was in the garden next door, but I wasn't ready to listen!"

Ada paused and said,

"Well, love, you are able to call them whenever you need to, and when it gets too much you are able to stop them too. In the business, we use seances as a way to stop them bothering us when we are not ready, sort of like a queuing system. When you want to talk to one you can go to their 'place', clearly for Anne the garden is one of her 'places' and call her. You don't have to say anything out loud, you do it with, well, with your spirit. What I mean is, she is probably waiting for you now. That's why Susan has been there when you wanted to talk to her."

Feeling the intense urgency of the situation, Maeve, who was already standing, took this in as she moved towards the french windows that opened directly onto the garden. One twist of the key and she pushed them open. She could already see Anne waiting for her, her arms hanging over the garden fence with her gardening gloves on.

"I know you weren't ready so I gave the message to Orla, she's a dear, so grown up now! I hope that was alright, I hope I didn't get her into any trouble?"

Maeve's stomach was in a knot, she really hoped Orla wasn't in trouble too, as she asked,

"What did you tell her exactly?"

"Well, I know who killed me. You remember, I started doing those classes up at the University on a Saturday morning? Local history, I learned so much, and the teacher or 'professor' was such a handsome man. When I was a bit lost on the campus, I knew that I knew him but I couldn't remember who he was.

"For a minute I thought he was my son Rupert and I went to give him a hug. He didn't like that. Told me to 'get away'. But in my mind he was Rupert so I wouldn't go away, how could he reject his mother? So I tried again, that's all I remember, except for the smell, that clean shaven, aftershave smell, that was the last thing I remember."

Maeve was shocked, but managed a stammering

"To be clear, was his name Tony, Tony Blackstone?"

"Yes, yes, that's him. Who would have thought such a nice

looking man would do that?" Anne shook her head ruefully, "Oh, and you need to know, the one you are looking for is still alive, at least I would know if he was dead and I can't feel him yet."

Maeve was completely stunned. For a few minutes she didn't say or do anything as she was playing it back in her mind. Then she dashed back to the house, shouting over her shoulder as she went

"Thank you Anne, I'll be back as soon as I can."

"I know dear, I know.", Anne said as she smiled, looking over the garden.

Maeve was hunting for her mobile phone, when Ada handed it to her,

"It was on the charger thing."

Within a few seconds Maeve had pulled up the image she was looking for, it was the photo with Susan and Kamal at the rocket society, and there standing behind them was a younger looking Tony Blackstone. What to do now?

The three women looked at each other.

Maeve took charge,

"Right, this is probably a police matter but they won't believe anything I say, so here's my plan. I go to the Cathedral, you wait outside, if I don't reappear in say fifteen minutes you call Steve on his mobile. Tell him all this, and tell him that we are missing and at high risk. He will have to do something, even if he doesn't want to."

Ada interjected, "There is no way I am waiting around for you. I am going in with you, if there are two of us at least I can be a distraction. Also if there are any spirits around you might need some help. And I won't collapse, I've been resting, I'm fine,"

Maeve nodded assent as she said

"Okay, everyone got their mobile phones? Let's go."

Having checked out the walking search of the campus, Steve had gone back to the station. As a detective he was meticulous, he liked order, facts, he often found that rereading files threw up information that had been overlooked in the heat of fresh leads. So he was laying out all the information that might be relevant, and some that might not be, but he had a hunch about.

He put Nigel Kennedy's version of Vivaldi's Four Seasons on his headphones to help block out the office noises, and clear his thinking while keeping up the pace. He had the file with the information on Susan's death which he knew by heart. Plus the new files that he had pulled together on Kamal.

Now he looked up suspicious deaths investigations and found one Kevin Dodds who was a senior University maintenance staff. Interesting that both Susan and Kevin had died of a broken neck, as had Anne. Were they linked? Was Kamal a red herring?

He printed out an enlarged photo of the group at the rocket launch that Maeve had sent him. He pinned that on the board that he was making, locating it on the large scale map of Canterbury from Google maps satellite view. He noticed that it was exactly the same location as where Anne's body had been found, strange.

CHAPTER 33

THE CATHEDRAL

Maeve had parked the car at the Burgate car park, tried to get in Queningate, but by now the gate was closed. They did a relatively swift walk down Burgate to the main Cathedral entrance.

Marianne had taken charge of logistics and police liaison, she was keen to get back-up as soon as possible. In passing Marianne gave her resident's pass to Ada, they might need to do some blagging, the passes always help, and she didn't need hers as she was going to wait outside in Buttermarket, ready to call Steve.

However Marianne needn't have bothered, Maeve wasn't going to let anyone stop her getting inside the Cathedral.

In fact it turned out to be surprisingly easy, once they mentioned Tony Blackstone the security guard only grumbled that

"They're supposed to tell us when there is an event on. There have been enough comings and goings this evening to classify it as an event",

and he thought he would take it up with Tony later, there would be overtime due.

The flood lighting makes the Cathedral stand out from its surrounding, ensuring it is visible for miles around. This evening however, they were in darkness, as the main lights had been switched off for repairs. Maeve and Ada walked through the archway, and across the open ground in front of the entrance with minimal illumination. Maeve steered them around passed the entrance to the Cathedral itself, passed the entrance to the Archbishop's residence, on to the cloisters. They went through the cloister, passed the entrance to the chapter house, Ada remarking,

"It's a good thing you know your way around here!"

Turning right after the chapter house there was a door on the left marked 'Archives and Library Reading Room.'

Maeve said,

"Fingers crossed this guy is a cocky bastard and has left the door unlocked."

They were indeed in luck, the grill and the door had both been left open, revealing the circular stone stairs winding up to the Reading room. Maeve had surmised that the staircase might also lead down. She led Ada round to the back of the staircase, and used her phone as a torch to light up the area, just as she had hoped, the discretely hidden set of steps going down came into view.

Marianne was standing in the middle of Buttermarket watching the timer on her phone. She was giving them the fifteen minutes Maeve had asked for, but not one second longer. She had saved Steve's number under 'A Steve' so that it was the first number in her contact list.

Of course they had tried calling, and messaging Orla, she could see that the messages hadn't gone through. So Orla didn't have any signal. Looking at her own signal, it was showing signal strength down to one bar. Shit. The middle of Canterbury is really bad for mobile signal so she backed up Mercery Lane keeping the entrance to the Cathedral in full view. She stood in the middle of the High Street, watching the Cathedral entrance. Ten minutes forty-five seconds left on the timer.

. . .

Maeve and Ada crept down the stairs as quietly as they could, but unlike in the movies, they did make noise, and the light was a dead giveaway. As they descended to level ground, they could see some light at the end of the short corridor. This was the only direction that they could go, so they followed the light and entered the spacious crypt under the Cathedral. They heard the metal click of a large old fashioned key turning in a lock, and the clunk as the mechanism locked in place, then they heard the disembodied voice,

"Welcome!"

Steve was still in the station ploughing through the files and testing his own theories. He tried some Google cross searches to see if they threw up any connections that he hadn't seen. The bizarre one that had appeared a few times had been archeology. He just couldn't see the fit, except for Adam, he was the only one connected to archeology. So he dismissed it.

Maeve had estimated that the lock was probably to secure the central area where the special collections were kept. She signaled to Ada to stay close behind her.

"We meet again, three times in one day, we must stop, or people will start talking."

Tony spoke as if they had just run into each other in the High Street. Maeve had already decided that he was a narcissistic psychopath so was channeling her most charming flirtatious self.

"I couldn't keep away. What wonderful secrets have you unearthed?"

She asked as if it was a normal enquiry. They moved towards the locked gate in the caged area that surrounded the precious display cases. Tony was standing in front of the gate with the keys in his hand. She glimpsed someone lying on the floor, and then saw Orla cradling their head, probably Adam, possibly still alive but probably in a coma. She knew that if she could keep him talking for long enough they had a chance. As they moved into the light, Tony looked at Ada,

"Ah, the famous, or should I say infamous, medium? What a pleasure to meet you. Shame I won't have the time to get to know you."

This gave Maeve an idea, sometimes you just have to go for broke.

Steve was still sitting there, running through the information, the details, cross referencing small details. He knew there was something there, right in front of him, if only he could see it. Thinking hard he pulled on his ear lobe, and then it hit him. It was looking at the photos of Susan. The earring. He had seen one just like that today, Tony Blackstone was wearing one. Then he looked up at the enlarged photo on the wall, and there he was standing behind Susan.

He rustled through the paperwork in front of him and sure enough the last person to see Kevin Dodd was Tony Blackstone. He was the link to archeology. More rustling and he found that Anne had signed up to Tony Blackstone's outreach classes on local history. He was the link to them all. Now the big question, 'where is he right now'? Unsurprisingly there was no reply from Tony's mobile.

Maeve had turned to Ada and winked, then back to Tony,

"Of course you know who you have here? Ada is the most famous medium because she can call any spirit and they must come to her. You know what that means? Who in the wide ranges of history would you most like to talk to?"

By the stillness of Tony's body she knew that she had caught his attention. So she went on,

"I mean, I don't know who you want to talk to, but I guess that we are here in the very place that Thomas a Becket was murdered. Wouldn't you want to talk to him?", she had hooked him. Ada now knew exactly what Maeve was driving at, what she wanted her to do, taking a deep breath Ada launched into,

"Of course you know that the spirit is strongest at the exact spot where they died, and if they were murdered, the blood can anchor their spirit to the place where it soaked into the ground."

Maeve took over with,

"I am not sure where that was, I mean there is a spot marked in the Cathedral but I have no idea if that is actually the right place."

"Well, there is a lot of post hoc justification, but still there is little doubt that he was pulled from the altar, so there or thereabouts, is the most likely spot",

Tony was beginning to take ownership of this adventure, his narcissistic nature would require it. Ada's sense of the drama was feeding him.

"Tony, darling, could you get hold of the biggest candle you can lay your hands on? Do we have any music of the era, that always helps the spirit find their way? What about the Allegri Miserere?"

"Don't be ridiculous, that's the 17th century! What we need is some plainchant, or some fabulous Hildegard von Bingen.", Tony was getting excited at the drama of the setting and the chance to actually meet Thomas a Becket. Ada knew that they had to keep this as Tony's drama, so asked,

"Do you know where Maeve could get some more candles? It would be great to bring the place alive?"

Marianne was looking at the time moving achingly slowly, then she thought, 'Mum's wrong about this'. And with the surge of confidence in taking control of her own decisions and with nine minutes left on her timer, she pressed Steve's number and waited.

. . .

Maeve had managed to pick up the keys, as Tony was organising the music to play in the Cathedral, she slid them under the bars of the grill coughing to hide the sound, with a

"Dusty down here", comment as she signalled to Orla to stay completely silent.

As soon as Steve answered the phone, Marianne started rambling with a roundabout explanation and justification, Steve interrupted

"Where is he now?"

He needed no further persuading as he had come to the same conclusion. The complicating factor was that Tony had three new potential victims. Steve had also put together that he was a psychopath, so killing them would not cause him a moment's doubt or hesitation. If the police arrived sirens blaring, it would make him kill, and, or, run. Neither was the best outcome, so this needed to be a silent operation.

There was only one 'crim', and as far as they knew he wasn't armed. Steve decided that if he called in the Cathedral security guards as guides and extra support in extremis, with his own men following asap that would be enough. He alerted his team, and asked them to meet up at the Cathedral Gate, silently. He had his radio and would call them in to place as needed. He also got a paramedic on standby.

He was with Marianne in less than five minutes. While parking his motorbike in the entrance he got the security guards up to speed. They were looking over towards the Cathedral mapping out potential exits, when they noticed there were flickering lights inside the main body of the Cathedral, and they could hear church music. What on earth was happening? Was he starting a fire? Call the fire dept, get the fire engines on standby.

Steve didn't think this was a wild goose chase, he didn't know what he was going to find inside, and he didn't want to be too late. So distributing the guards at the exits, he gave instructions to his team. Marianne wasn't going to wait this time, she was sticking close to Steve. Steve decided to enter via the Knights door, the very entrance that the four knights had used to murder Thomas a Becket. This door is the closest to the altar in the centre of the building, so the best bet for a relatively discrete entrance.

Inside the Cathedral they had encouraged Tony to play the music as loud as he would dare, and had given him the largest candle to hold as he sat in the archbishops enthronement seat, with the idea that he was guiding the spirit to them. Meanwhile Maeve had lit as many of the votive candles around the Cathedral as she could. The effect was magical. And if the plan worked, it would alert Steve, and the police to their location.

Ada noticed Orla creeping up behind Tony. So drawing his attention towards herself she started her 'incantations',

"An bhfuil cead agam dul amach le do thoil, Thomas a Beachead ….", banking on the likelihood that Tony didn't speak or understand Irish Gaelic, because she certainly didn't speak any latin. Maeve saw what she was doing and decided that now was the time. Tony was sitting in the Chair of St Augustine presiding over the nave, holding the giant candle aloft in front of him. Maeve had been going around the Cathedral lighting candles and laying a circle of candles around his feet, she slipped behind him, and went for the biggest lump of metal that she could find, which was the Amnesty candle holder. She crept up behind him as the music echoed and hit him as hard as she could on the back of the head.

When Steve, with Marianne behind him, walked through the door, it took them a moment to assess the scene in front of them. The Cathedral was ethereal in candle light with the sonorous plainchant filling the space. As their eyes adjusted to the soft light they could see Tony lying unconscious on the floor, and the three women standing there, Maeve with a giant candlestick in her hands. Marianne ran up the altar steps and in seconds all four were hugging each other, whilst doing a little dance.

CHAPTER 34

THE WRAP UP

Orla was with the paramedic when they got the insulin into Adam, he was still alive, but full recovery would take some time. Even comatose Orla thought she had been right when she saw him in the admissions office, he was cute; she might have found a reason to be happy to stay in Canterbury for a while.

Steve stayed with the unconscious Tony, until the medic had treated him too and he began to come around. At which point Steve arrested him. Steve's team were there, the officers had taken the candlestick in case it would be needed as evidence. Tim's search team had been called off.

Steve said to Maeve,

"You might have killed him. That's one hell of a weapon."

Maeve was so relieved that she was almost silly,

"I just didn't want him to get up again. I don't know how to fight and what would I do if he came after me?"

When the women had regrouped in the nave of the Cathedral, they were all talking over each other, filling in the missing bits, excited and relieved. Orla asked Ada,

"What were the incantations? I have never heard you do anything like that before."

At this both Maeve and Ada almost collapsed laughing.

"Well," said Ada struggling hard to get the words out while laughing so hard, "I don't actually know any incantations and I took a chance that Tony wouldn't understand any of the Irish language so I said the first thing that came into my head,"

Ada had to take a break as she was hiccuping giggles

"It's what we used to say in school," pause, "I asked if I could go to the toilet."

The laughter was so infectious that even if it wasn't that funny they all roared with that belly laughter that is hard to stop.

The next day was a Monday, it should have been a school day. But this Monday neither Marianne nor Orla were going anywhere. They were blocked in by another media storm. The word had got out that they had been kidnapped and the kidnapper was the potential killer. Clearly this was the follow up to the previous media storm and now they had a story with a relatively happy ending. They weren't going away anytime soon. Maeve feared that there would be a lot of explaining to do with the other neighbours. But as it turned out some of them were actually enjoying the sudden interest in their now celebrity neighbours, and were happy to talk,

"always such nice people, I never would have thought…"

Learning from Ruth, Maeve had suggested that they draft an official statement and try to manage the press. She was aware that this level of exposure could change their lives and media intrusion was not something Maeve welcomed. This time she brought Marianne and Orla into the conversation. Marianne was confident,

"Please keep me out of this if you can. I want to get on with my studies and go to college in the autumn, I don't want this story to follow me."

Orla was equally opinionated and in complete agreement

"No one will take me seriously as a protestor if they know I can talk to ghosts. So don't mention me either. In fact maybe Marianne and I should go to Ada's as a hideout?."

Edward whispered into Maeve's ear

"She still can't see me, m'lady!" making Maeve smile which Orla took as a yes.

Having arranged it as agreed, and just before they went to do the press statement, Maeve said to Ada,

"What was it that you wanted to tell me yesterday? You said that there was one more important piece of information."

Ada hesitated,

"Well it's not so urgent now but you probably should know. Ever since the heart attack, I have not spoken to a spirit. None of them have tried to contact me. I think I felt so close to death myself that I shut them out. I don't know if I want to open that door again. I don't need it anymore, I have truly begun to reconnect with you. The spirit world came to me for family healing. I didn't realise that I was helping them instead of dealing with my own family."

She had her hand on Maeve's arm. She stopped thoughtfully and said to Maeve,

"With you it's different, they know what you are good at, they are coming to you to solve injustices."

Maeve was uncertain,

"I did wonder if something was going on when you weren't sharing any messages from the other side. However let's not take anything for granted just yet. We have a lot of our own family relationships to work our way through, between us and with two emerging young women who need our help to find themselves."

They were looking at each other both in contemplation, Maeve broke the silence first,

"I have just had a thought, and I have a big question to ask you….. would you be alright dealing with the media on your own? I'd rather you were the front man and you could keep me out of the picture. Marianne and Orla have already disappeared, maybe I could too? I don't want the press attention and you're already famous. Remember what Steve said to us, 'the press never let the truth get in the way of a good story.' So use it, and give them a good story!."

"Oh shit!"

Maeve hadn't waited for a reply; she could see the delight on Ada's face, and knew that Ada would be in her element creating the drama.

"I just remembered Anne is waiting to talk to me. You will be brilliant Ada. Make it great." Maeve winked at her mother as she slipped out the back, saying

"We *are* a great team."

The days that followed were a blur, the media interest was insane, Ada did take the lead and the others enjoyed seeing her shine. No interviews for Simon though, Ada wasn't going to forgive him for some time. Now as a protector of their secrets and with the support of her *whole* family to come back to, Ada embraced her new beginning.

Ray was slowly coming to terms with the fact that Anne was not going to come back. The relief of not having to keep her dementia a secret, and of not watching her decline, was competing with guilt, and overwhelmingly with the sadness of the loss of his best friend. Throughout all of this Ruth was amazing, in fact Maeve could see herself in Ruth's actions. Ruth was sorting everyone else out because she herself wasn't ready to face the loss of her mother yet. That would come in time, when she was surrounded by her family, probably when they were all back in Egypt. Rupert had arrived from Australia, the retelling of the story seemed to help them all. Their grieving was a blend of crying, and then remembering something funny, and laughing. The laughter might look callous to an outsider but it united the family, and it was what Anne would have wanted.

In fact it was what she wanted, Anne told Maeve while Maeve was out weeding in the garden, and Maeve promised to pass it on.

Maeve was considering what to do about all of the messages and requests, Susan and Kamal in particular. Ada suggested that Maeve take a pause for a while, and then when the media had moved on, Maeve could check in on them. Sometimes the actions on their own would release the spirits, and sometimes they needed more, but as spirits they were not in a rush, it could wait till Maeve was ready.

Maeve had finally had the time to take Edward aside and say,

"Please stop calling me m'lady, my name is Maeve."

He bowed and said,

"Lady Maeve, it shall be."

Edward refused to listen to her further protestations on the basis that he had no intention of becoming a second class servant, he was no uncouth day labourer so it was Lady Maeve, or he would have to consider his position. Equally Maeve had no intention of losing his help, and decided that becoming Lady Maeve inside her own home, and known only to herself was probably fine.

Anne's funeral was that Friday, her family had gathered. Maeve, Ada, Marianne, Orla (and Edward) had got together to bake cakes, make finger food, and provide endless supplies of tea.

Steve appeared behind Maeve and broke into her revery with

"Any more of that tea? I'm parched."

"You almost made me jump! You will have to wait till the kettle boils."

Maeve was sharp but with a laugh in her voice. Steve went on as if they had been in the middle of a conversation,

"You know that saying, I think it was Eleanor Roosevelt's, 'a woman is like a tea bag you don't know how strong she is until you put her in hot water.' All I can say is, you four women make strong tea, and if I was ever in a pickle I'd be happy to have any one of you by my side."

He was looking straight at Maeve as he spoke, and his eyes twinkled.

Ruth was sitting in Maeve's kitchen resting her feet for a moment, waiting for the latest batch from the oven.

"You know, Mum would have loved this. So many of her friends came, and all the work that you have done has made it feel almost like a party. I am sure she would have enjoyed that and seeing everyone in her garden."

Ruth sighed. Maeve wasn't quite sure how to put it,

"Actually she is enjoying it. But really, most of all, she wants you to know that she is happy. She won't leave until all of you are ready. She asked, if in time, you would help your father to find a friend. She said, not a replacement, just someone to do things with, 'he's not good on his own.' "

Ruth beamed,

"Oh Maeve, I really needed to hear that. It helps so much. Can you tell her how much I love her and miss her?"

"She knows", said Maeve as she gave Ruth a hug, "and remember we're always here for you too."

"Actually Maeve, there is something I meant to tell you. You know that Dad is going to come and visit us in Egypt. Well I have asked Ada if she would come too, it will be in a little while. I hope that's okay with you? I know that Dad is not a good traveller so it would be great if they could travel together. And I don't want to leave without having something to look forward to."

. . .

Anne had asked Maeve not to talk to Ray yet, 'He will need it when they have all gone, he's not ready to hear from me, it will be better when there is no one else around.'

As Ruth left the kitchen with the tray of hot food, Maeve thought back to that day in Margate, now she really understood the value of her gift. She was sure that there would be more to come.

MAEVE'S RECIPES

Maeve's recipe for Irish Brown Soda Bread - sometimes called Wheaten Bread.

'Maeve started the day with a spring in her step. The house was ready, she would do the grocery shopping on her way over to the hospital in Ashford. What to feed Ada? Start with comfort food, baked potatoes and homemade coleslaw, no grated cheese or minimal butter, should be okay and easy to prepare. Or something an invalid could eat, homemade brown bread with a boiled egg? That would do it, it was Maeve's own favourite food when she needed to recover from anything.'

350g brown flour
175g white flour
100g bran
50g wheat germ
100g pinhead oats
1 teaspoon bread soda (bicarbonate of soda)
½ teaspoon salt
550-600ml buttermilk
200ml water or more to make the mixture liquid

Use a 2lb (23x13cm) rectangular bread tin, grease it well. Mix the dry ingredients in a large bowl, add the liquid, mix with your hand in a 'claw shape' so have the minimum contact with the mix (no kneading!). It works best when it's not too dry so you can add water as needed. Cook in the oven at gas 3, or 160⁰C (or 140⁰C fan oven) for an hour to 1hour 15mins until it is brown on top and beginning to come away from the sides.

When you take it out of the oven, turn it out onto a wire tray to allow the bottom to dry out.

Additions:

Sesame seeds - sprinkled over the top, use a spoon or a fork to press them in slightly to keep them in place

Sunflower seeds, pumpkin seeds, flaxseed (also called linseed), hemp seed all or some of which can be added to the bread, I usually add a scattering of each one (or whatever is in the cupboard).

~

Maeve's Quick Raspberry Jam. (It takes about 20mins from start to your own jam)

'Marianne had found the homemade brown bread in the freezer, made toast and coffee, plus of course Barry's tea for Ada, Orla adding her own favourite raspberry jam from the garden.'

Pick your raspberries and slightly under ripe are better than over ripe ones. Rinse the fruit and then weigh it. You will need half the weight of fruit in sugar so 200g raspberries plus 100g sugar. This is less sugar that traditional recipes with would have equal weight of sugar to fruit.

Prepare the jar you are going to use to store the jam in.

Put the raspberries in a stainless steel saucepan and heat for 3-4mins until the juice begins to run. Bring them up to boiling point, then add the sugar. Now reduce the heat and stir over a gentle heat until the sugar has dissolved. Bring the heat back up and boil steadily for 5 or 6 minutes stirring frequently. You can test it at this stage to see if it will set by putting a teaspoon of the jam onto a cold plate and seeing if any wrinkles form on the surface. When it sets enough for your taste (remember it has been boiling while you do the test so will be a little further on), pour into your jam jars. Cover immediately.

~

Making Tea.

'Ada agreed to mind the house, or more likely 'phone sit' and settled in with her fresh pot of tea,'

A lot of people from Ireland like strong black tea and there is no mystery in the making of it, however there is often some dispute over tea bags or loose leaf tea. Maeve had found this great invention of 'tea socks', like a giant empty tea bag that you can fill yourself. Ada preferred the tea she had grown up with, and was used to tea bags from the Irish brand 'Barry's'. What they agreed on was how to make it.

Boil water. Heat the teapot by adding some of the boiling water and swirling it around in the pot, then empty it out. If you are using a mug don't bother with preheating it, it's unlikely to get too cold. Add your tea, either loose leaf or tea bags, traditionally it's a teaspoon of tea leaves per person and 'one for the pot', but that may be a bit strong depending on your taste. Pour the now slightly cooled water from the kettle over the tea and leave to stand for at least a minute or two, some say 4 minutes, until the brew is a good strong dark but clear colour. If there is a film or some scum on the surface this is usually due to 'hard' water with high levels of lime in it. Filtered water will make the tea taste better, especially if you are in Canterbury.

Pour, add milk or lemon or whatever you like for a good cup of tea.

MAP OF THE CANTERBURY MURDERS

Appendix II. The Map

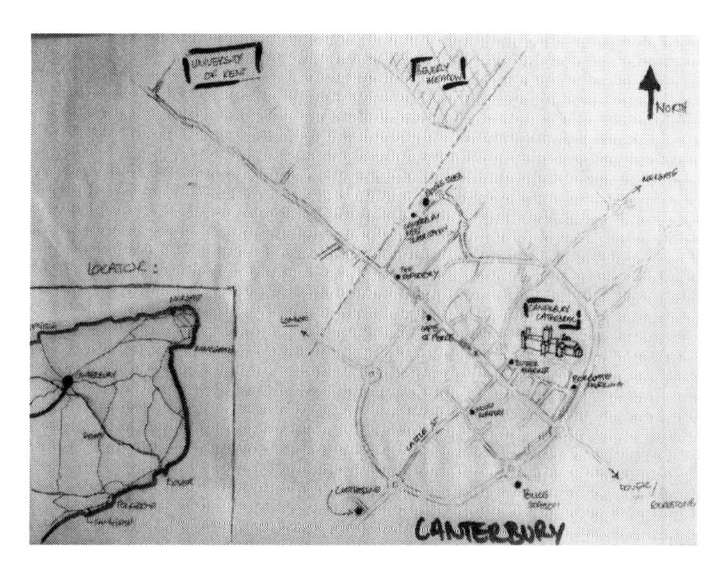

Printed in Great Britain
by Amazon

63420605R00128